Praise

"Burnsworth nails the author will win you over then keep you turning pages with his suspense."

– Hank Phillippi Ryan,
Mary Higgins Clark Award-Winning Author of *Say No More*

"Hop on board for a hard-edged debut that's fully loaded with car chases (particularly Mustangs), war veterans, old grudges, and abundant greed. A choppy start belies a well-executed plotline enhanced by the atmospheric Palmetto State setting."

– *Library Journal*

"This second case for Brack is marked by a challenging mystery, quirky characters, and nonstop action."

– *Kirkus Reviews*

"In Brack Pelton, Burnsworth introduces a jaded yet empathetic character I hope to visit again and again."

– Susan M. Boyer,
Agatha Award-Winning Author of *Lowcountry Book Club*

"Burnsworth is outstanding as he brings out the heat, the smells, the colors, and the history of Charleston during Pelton's mission to bring the killer to justice."

– John Carenen,
Author of *A Far Gone Night*

"If you have always suspected there is more to Charleston than quaint Southern charm and ghost stories, then David Burnsworth's noir series, featuring ex-soldier, tiki bar owner, and part time beach bum, Brack Pelton may just be the antidote to a surfeit of sweet tea."

– Michael Sears,
Shamus Award-Winning Author of *Black Fridays*

BAD TIME
TO BE IN IT

Books by David Burnsworth

The Blu Carraway Mystery Series

BLU HEAT (Prequel Novella)
IN IT FOR THE MONEY (#1)
BAD TIME TO BE IN IT (#2)

The Brack Pelton Mystery Series

SOUTHERN HEAT (#1)
BURNING HEAT (#2)
BIG CITY HEAT (#3)

BAD TIME TO BE IN IT

A BLU CARRAWAY MYSTERY

DAVID BURNSWORTH

HENERY PRESS

Copyright

BAD TIME TO BE IN IT
A Blu Carraway Mystery
Part of the Henery Press Mystery Collection

First Edition | July 2018

Henery Press, LLC
www.henerypress.com

Trade Paperback ISBN-13: 978-1-63511-358-7
Digital epub ISBN-13: 978-1-63511-359-4
Kindle ISBN-13: 978-1-63511-360-0
Hardcover ISBN-13: 978-1-63511-361-7

Printed in the United States of America

For Patty

ACKNOWLEDGMENTS

This book would not have come together without the tireless efforts of Christina Rogers and many others at Henery Press and my publicist Row Carenen. They helped shape the book into one of my favorites. All the fan praise should be directed their way, while any flaws found within are mine alone.

Jill Marr of the Sandra Dijkstra Literary Agency has my complete trust. I am in good hands with her.

Just as they did for the previous Blu Carraway Book, *In It For The Money*, my parents, Mom and Ron, gave this book a thorough review. Thanks so much for your tireless support of my writing endeavor.

Two new beta readers emerged this time around: Cheryl Sherman and John Norris. Cheryl, thanks for your willingness to give unbiased suggestions. John, thanks so much for being a fan and for offering to give it a preview!

My wife, Patty, sacrifices so much for me. I couldn't ask for a better companion in this life.

As always, the South Carolina Writers Association deserves credit for helping me to be a published author. Aspiring writers in South Carolina should make this organization their first stop on the way to any publication goals they have.

Finally, thanks to all you readers. You are the reason I keep writing.

God Bless!

Chapter One

Paco squinted as he stared out over the courtyard, the afternoon sun a brilliant blaze. Sounds of local women selling vegetables, cheap pottery, and trinkets to tourists filled the air. The clinking of dishware. Some of the vendors were lucky enough to have an umbrella or canopy to shield them from the burning heat. Most weren't.

The pavement baked Paco's feet through his cowboy boots.

He lifted his straw hat, one with an orange band he'd bought from a local Mennonite child, and wiped his brow. The air tasted of salt, dust, and tamalito grease.

His two partners, a Belizean Creole called Lin and a Jamaican named Peter, were already in position. Lin nodded at him from the other side of the square. Paco checked on Peter and found him fifty meters due east scoping out the three young women they'd come for.

Well, really it was just one of them they wanted. The other two women were going to be a bonus. The contract was to grab the woman with the family name of Kincaid, make a phone call when they had her at their hideout, and then do whatever they wanted with the other two. And eliminate any resistance.

The stupid chicas had only one guard with them. Some tall, middle-aged Bufon Paco guessed was half-Cuban, half-gringo, who wore sunglasses and dressed in light-colored fatigues and military-style boots. He looked fit but was most likely nothing but an easy target. In the three days Peter, Lin, and Paco had tracked the women, the man with the sunglasses always kept watch from behind.

The past two nights Paco had dreamt of shooting the man through those sunglasses.

Using the sleeve of his shirt, Paco wiped his forehead one more time and then replaced his hat. He watched Peter wait until the women and the man passed and then fell in behind them.

God, the women were beautiful. Suntanned white girls in their early twenties. Perfect teeth. Curled, long hair. Linen blouses, short shorts, and sandals. After he shot their protector, his dreams ended with tying each of them to a bed, the fear in their eyes giving him immense pleasure.

And today was the day his dream would come true.

Paco watched the group pass through a crowd of old people in bright clothes unloading from a tour bus.

Except Peter didn't emerge behind them when the women came through the other side of the gray-haired mass.

Neither did the sunglass-wearing guard.

Paco smiled and thought, good, Peter took him out already.

He nodded at Lin who gave him a thumbs-up.

The women perused another row of vendors.

He and Lin followed, coming from opposite ends.

The women were just ahead. Paco caught sight of their toned caderas and thanked his god again for tight American shorts. He picked up his pace as he threaded through the crowd.

After about forty meters, something didn't seem right any more. He should have caught up to them by now. And Lin should have joined him.

Paco stopped, checked his phone. No messages.

Looking around, he thought he spotted the women turn down an alley.

Where were Peter and Lin?

It didn't matter.

Today was the day.

He had to get the woman now. Especially with the guard out of the picture.

Paco knew he could handle her by himself, even if the other two females had to die to make things easier. He sprinted after them, cut down the alley, and found himself alone with nothing but a dead end. The only noise he heard was the market from which he'd come.

An abandoned car on blocks with its hood open mocked him. Dust kicked up from his boots as he skidded to a stop. Paco turned around. No one had followed him.

He turned back and looked straight down the barrel of a revolver.

His eyes would not—could not—keep from staring at the black hole in front of him that brought death. Where in the hell did this come from? There had been no sound.

A man's voice said, "*Esto es donde dar la vuelta y a pie.*" (This is where you turn around and walk away.)

Thinking fast, Paco said, "*Que buscaba para mi hija.*" (I was looking for my daughter.)

The thumb of the hand holding the revolver cocked the hammer back.

Anyone else would have soiled his pants at this. But Paco knew the man had made a very big mistake. Other peoples' mistakes, and Paco's awareness of them, were how he had survived this long. The cocked pistol an arm's reach from his face had caught him off guard. If it had been five feet away, the perfect distance for control, he would have had a problem.

But this close—

Paco swung an arm at the hand with the pistol and ducked the other way, all in one motion just like he'd done before.

Except another gun fired.

Paco felt an inferno of heat and lead tear through his leg. He screamed and crashed to the ground.

A large, military boot kicked him in the face. It jolted his focus off the pain in his leg for a second and onto the sunglasses of the man from his dreams. Paco spotted a second pistol in the man's other hand. He hadn't seen the second gun because he couldn't tear his eyes away from the first. The man had outsmarted him.

The man smiled down at him and said, in Spanish, "Who hired you?"

The pain flooded back. Paco seethed out a "Piss off."

The man with the sunglasses put his large boot on Paco's injured leg and stepped down hard.

Paco had never felt pain so great in his thirty-three years on this earth. He tried to scream, but nothing came out. He swam in a horizon of white noise.

The pressure on his leg let up. The boot kicked him in the ribs, ripping his concentration away from his leg once more, long enough for him to breathe.

"Your two friends won't be joining us. Tell me who hired you. Do it now. I won't ask again."

Paco's mind recovered enough from the pain to formulate a last desperate plan. He slipped a hand behind his back and pulled out a derringer.

Before he could aim it, the man standing over him blasted his hand from two feet away. And Paco felt a different twinge of pain that almost matched the firestorm in his leg. He lifted his hand to where he could look at it. Two of his fingers were missing.

Then he saw nothing.

Chapter Two

Mick Crome sat on a stool at the inside bar of the Pirate's Cove on the Isle of Palms. He finished off a second pint while staring at all the liquor bottles lined up on the shelves in front of him. They had a habit of staring back. Maureen, his sometimes girlfriend and bartender a hundred miles north up in Myrtle Beach, was pissed off at him. He couldn't chill and watch her tight rear end as she poured drinks tonight. Maybe not tomorrow night, either.

The current bartender serving the beers, a friend named Brack Pelton, wasn't exactly his type. At six feet and with a perpetual suntanned complexion, Brack looked like he should be tending bar in the Bahamas, not owning two watering holes in the South Carolina lowcountry.

Pelton asked, "You want another one, Mick?"

Even inside the place, the smell of the Atlantic Ocean directly behind him cleaned out his sinuses. The song streaming on the bar's sound system, "Paradise City" by Guns and Roses, was a real classic.

Crome nodded, hooked a boot heel on the bottom rung of his stool, and pulled a vape pen out of the breast pocket of his weathered leather vest.

He couldn't figure out what exactly he'd done wrong with Maureen but was sure it might have something to do with the two women he traded vodka shots with the night before. Mainly because neither of them was Maureen.

Maureen hadn't taken too kindly to him cancelling their date so he could follow a lead only to end up getting drunk and crashing at another woman's pad. She didn't believe him when he'd tried to explain that nothing had happened. The lead was legit, but even he knew he should have just gotten the information over the phone.

What did people say in times like this? C'est la vie?

Whatever.

Pelton set a fresh pint of draft down in front of Crome. "Haven't seen you or Blu around in a while. How's it going?"

The kid, Pelton, meant well. If Crome hadn't taken a liking to him, and if he hadn't watched a video of the kid, empty handed, take on an armed giant of a man and win, he might have picked a fight with him just for fun. But the kid had saved his best friend's daughter and was an unofficial partner in the private investigation firm Crome co-owned. Unofficial because just about everything Crome did was unofficial. The official side was handled by his main partner, Blu Carraway.

Crome said, "Blu's on a security job. In Belize, the lucky bastard. Should be back in a day or two."

A voice from behind him said, "Hi, Crome."

It was female and familiar. Damn.

Anyone else would have been a welcome change to his wandering thoughts, a defense mechanism he used to avoid thinking about Maureen.

Hell, Maureen in her most pissed-off state would have been a welcome companion compared to—

The female voice interrupted his thought. "Aren't you going to invite me to sit down?"

Crome saw the smirk form on his own face reflected in the mirror behind the bar. He also saw the strawberry-blond curls, red lipstick, and tight dress of his newest problem. "It's a free country."

Harmony Childs pulled out the stool next to him and sat. "That bad-ass biker routine won't work on me, Sugar. You've seen me in my underwear."

Twenty years his junior, nuttier than a pecan tree, driven, and drop-dead gorgeous, Harmony was the very cliché of Kryptonite for him. She was also one of the two women he'd traded shots with last night.

It was true; he had seen her in her underwear. But not out of her underwear, thank God, or he and Maureen wouldn't have lasted this long.

Harmony said, "Don't tell me you've still got a hangover. I'd hate to think you couldn't hang with us, given your propensity for bars and liquor."

She really was beautiful. And she'd matched him shot for shot, unless the bartender was feeding her and her friend water instead of Citron. But that couldn't be because he'd watched all their shot glasses get refilled from the same bottle.

"Not on your life, Dolly," he said.

Pelton came over, grinned at the young woman, and said, "What'll it be, Ms. Harmony?"

If Pelton's wife caught him doing anything more than casual flirting, she'd string him up by his testicles. Especially if it was with Harmony. Or her cohort, Tess Ray. Which reminded Crome, when there was one, the other wasn't far behind.

Tess pulled out the stool on the other side of Crome and sat. "Sorry I'm late. There was another double homicide in North Charleston."

Shorter than Harmony, with shoulder length blonde hair that fell in layers, Tess wore dark-rimmed glasses, a business dress with no sleeves, and medium heels.

She'd been the second woman from the night before. Two women to one man, a bottle of vodka, and all he had to show for it was a nasty headache, a stiff back from the couch he'd crashed on alone, and a pissed off girlfriend. Must be his lucky day.

Crome opened his mouth to say "howdy" but got cut off before he could start.

"It would be nice if your partner was around," Harmony said.

"You guys make good copy. Maybe you all could give us something besides gang violence to report on."

Harmony and Tess were eager-beaver news correspondents who'd recently gone independent.

Tess asked, "So when is Blu due back in town? Soon, right?"

Every damn woman who'd ever laid eyes on Blu Carraway fell in love with the bastard.

Again, Crome opened his mouth to speak, and again got interrupted. This time by the other local lady killer, Pelton's dog, Shelby.

At the sight of the chow-collie mix, Harmony and Tess both slid off their stools and swarmed the mutt. The damned canine seemed to be eating it all up, dancing around between them, his wagging tail high in the air.

The song ended, and in the lull before the next one began, Crome checked his iPhone, the one that felt like an old-fashioned pair of handcuffs restraining him from freedom. The one that came with the business of running a private investigation firm. The one that his partner had made him take.

He'd missed a call.

The number wasn't familiar, but whoever had called left a voicemail. He listened.

It sounded like Maureen. "Mick? I'm in trouble. Please help—"

A man's voice cut her off. "Listen Crome, it's payback time. You took from me so I'm taking from you. I'll be in touch."

His phone showed a text message. He tapped to open it up and stared at a picture of a scared Maureen with a gun to her head.

Billy Idol's "Eyes Without a Face" started playing, blowing a hole through the world.

Chapter Three

Blu Carraway couldn't waste any more time with the man named Paco bleeding out at his feet. A gunshot wound to the femoral artery caused death inside of five minutes and the man was going fast. The women were still vulnerable even though Blu felt confident there were only the three adversaries. The stubborn man below him had been the last one standing.

Blu slid the revolver down the waistband of his pants, retrieved his iPhone from a pocket, and selected a number from the recent call feed. Their driver, a contractor Blu used from time to time, answered.

Blu asked, "The three bears eating their porridge?"

"Affirmative."

That meant the women were safe in the car with the driver.

"Can you see my location on the tracker?"

"Be there in ten seconds."

It had been a tough couple of days. Blu had spotted the tail after they docked the yacht in the harbor and came ashore. And now the immediate risk was over and they could head out to sea again, although the reason for the attempted ambush eluded him.

Blu said, "Come and get me."

He pressed end and the phone buzzed, signaling an incoming call. Blu looked at the display and answered. "Hey, Harmony."

She said, "You need to get back to Charleston. Now."

* * *

Tuesday morning
DAY TWO

After saying a brief goodbye to Jennifer Kincaid and her friends and handing them off to one of Jennifer's father's local bodyguards, Blu toted his gear from the G6 private jet to his black Nissan Xterra. The call from Harmony about Maureen's kidnapping had not been what he wanted to come home to. And the phone call to Crome had not gone any better. He'd been in a rage.

Blu and Crome both knew they had made many enemies over the years. This could be from any of them. Especially Crome, who did not hesitate to take things up a few notches to get whatever he needed. Blu preferred a little more finesse, but Crome never walked away empty handed.

Lately, Crome had taken residence at a rental that overlooked the ocean on Folly Beach. The owner of the home, an old friend, gave him a reasonable rate in return for watching over the place while he and his wife traveled abroad.

The neighbors probably didn't appreciate the loud motorcycle, but otherwise Blu suspected Crome kept to himself.

Blu had a key and entered through the front door. He and Crome had been brothers-in-arms for over twenty years. There were few boundaries.

Crome sat on the back deck staring at the Atlantic Ocean drinking from a cup of coffee and not busting heads, his normal MO.

He also preferred beer. And he liked to drink late into the night, even now in his forties. Yet here he was drinking coffee. The situation with Maureen seemed to have derailed him.

A derailed Mick Crome was something Blu had never seen before. The man prided himself on being cool and collected without an Achilles heel—until now.

Blu said, "How's it going?"

Ignoring the question, Crome asked, "How was Belize?"

"Not bad." Blu took a seat on a plastic chair next to his business partner.

"Nice work for the money," Crome said, "watching three twenty-year-olds sunbathe and shop all day."

Blu removed the pistol and holster from his belt and set the rig on the table between them. "So, how do you want to play this?"

Crome looked over at him. "It's my problem. Not yours."

"No wonder we get along so well," Blu said. "I tried that line on Billie last year and she told me to go pound sand. I'mma tell you the same thing. Then we're going to find Maureen and make an example of whoever took her."

"No need for you to get dirty on this one, Blu. I got a feeling karma's come to visit."

Blu put his hand on his partner's shoulder. "We'll get her back."

He tried to shrug it off. "Damn right I am."

"No, my friend," Blu said. "*We* are."

To their right, a set of stairs off the back deck led to the beach. Harmony and Tess crested the top of them just as Blu finished his statement. Harmony crossed her arms. "We all are."

Tess nodded. "That's right."

Crome shook his head. "I don't need you yahoos slowing me down."

That was definitely not the right thing to say to the young news correspondents who'd befriended them last year. Even if Harmony had gotten pissed off at Crome, showed her tail, almost got him beat up, and definitely got herself shot. But that was then. Now, the women and Crome and Blu were thick as thieves. Especially since the women had resigned from the *Palmetto Pulse* newspaper and had gone freelance.

They made a hell of a lot more money now doing commercials and YouTube video news updates. Since they'd cut their teeth at places like the Pulse and were known by everyone in Charleston County, no one questioned their media credentials.

Blu thought about hiring them, but realized having them around more than they already were probably wasn't a good idea. At least as far as he and his girlfriend, Billie, were concerned. Things had cooled since Blu had proposed and Billie had left town before his Belize job, telling him she needed time to take care of her sick mother and think.

"Now listen, Mick," Harmony said. "I know you and Mr. Blu over here wouldn't leave us hanging. We're in this together. No one messes with any of us. And that is that."

Tess said, "So send us the picture and let's get to work."

Blu was proud of them.

The first stop Blu made after Crome took off to Myrtle Beach and the women left to track down their own sources was to Phineous Soloman, Charleston's crackerjack photo analyzer. Blu watched the pale, lanky man work on the picture of Maureen in his makeshift office located in a rundown strip mall in North Charleston. His stringy hair and bad complexion didn't help his appearance.

"So what I can tell you," Phineous said, "is that there's nothing fake about it that I can find."

"Any observations?" Blu asked.

"Yeah," Phineous said, "whoever took the picture knew what they were doing—white walls, scared woman, gun to the head. No markings on the gun that I can find. You probably know it's a Glock."

Blu leaned in. "Any birth marks on the hand holding it?"

"None that I can see. It's his right hand."

"You're sure it's a man?"

"Not positive," Phineous said. "I'd say maybe sixty-five percent."

"Scarring? Tats? Anything?"

"Looks like he, or she, is a nail biter. Check out those ragged digits."

Phineous worked the mouse and keypad. He zoomed in on

Maureen's eyes. Then he zoomed in again, first on the left eye, which didn't show anything. But when he moved to the right eye and zoomed in further, something in the glare came into partial focus.

He said, "Might have something here."

"I thought that only worked in the movies."

Phineous smiled. "Digital photography is a wonderful thing. Give me some time and I'll work on cleaning up the image. Maybe I can tell you something more later."

Blu patted him on the back. "Phin, you're the man."

Not sure of what to do next, Blu called Harmony and Tess and they agreed to meet downtown at the Terrace rooftop bar.

Vaping while he waited, Blu looked out over Marian Square and thought things through. The statue of Francis Marian, the Swamp Fox, stood proud over the grass field. The last time Crome got this wound up he was popping four reds a day. There weren't any signs he'd backslid into pills, but these situations could be tricky. And they could certainly mess with a man's head.

The women showed up, both beautiful but neither happy.

Harmony said, "I've burned four chits and haven't come up with anything."

Chits in their lingo meant favors. For some reason, both ladies had an endless supply of them all over the city, even after they stopped reporting the news in an official capacity.

Tess said, "I talked to three people and got nowhere. I even talked to Darcy and still nothing."

Darcy was the wife of Brack Pelton, the owner of the Pirate's Cove bar on the Isle of Palms. She worked for her family's business, Wells Shipping, as head of their marketing and promotion efforts. But before that, she had been the most successful news correspondent in Charleston with sources all over the lowcountry. If she didn't know anything, then it was safe to assume no one else in Charleston County did, either.

Maureen lived alone in Myrtle Beach since her son went off to the Navy. As far as Blu could tell, she and Crome were an on-again, off-again item, mostly due to Crome being Crome and wanting his sole legal relationship to be with his motorcycle.

Blu said, "Phineous might be able to tell us something."

Harmony looked at Tess and then both eyed Blu.

Tess said, "We are not going to visit, call, date, or so much as be in any kind of close proximity to Phineous Solomon. Is that clear?"

Blu held up his hands. "No one's asking you to."

"Not yet," Harmony said. "But it will only be a matter of time before he does."

Tess nodded. "Just like the last time."

"Okay, now," Blu said, "the last time all he wanted was to receive the check from you two."

"In person," Harmony said. "Yuck."

"Don't try to pimp us out again," Tess said.

"Yeah," Harmony said. "Even if it is for Crome. We have our limits."

Chapter Four

Tuesday

Mick Crome rode fast and hard to Myrtle Beach and pulled into the gravel parking lot of Bert's, the dive bar where Maureen worked. The day was hot, the sky clear of any shading clouds.

He dropped the kickstand and leaned the bike onto it.

Before he approached anybody, he had to get his head screwed on straight. Seeing the fear in Maureen's eyes and knowing that it was because of him was something he had to put aside for the moment.

Whoever took Maureen was egging him on. They might even be scoping out the place, waiting for him to show.

His boots crunched on the gravel lot as he walked over to the building which consisted of two shipping containers welded together with the sides cut out. The smell of the ocean, even two miles inland, enveloped him.

Bert Dorman, the owner who looked a lot like Crome except two decades older, approached. He had a thick mustache that trailed down the sides of his mouth and connected to a week-old beard. A biker do-rag held back long, scraggly hair.

Dorman and Crome had ridden together in the nineties, raising hell all over the lowcountry. That was before Crome got serious with Blu about their investigation business. Well, really it was Blu's business. Crome preferred it that way.

He and Dorman shook hands with an arm-wrestler's grip and

then let go.

Dorman asked, "You holding up?"

"Not really," Crome said. "When was the last time you seen her?"

"She worked last night and then I get the call from you at noon." Dorman put his hand on Crome's shoulder. "I'm all tore up about it."

"Anything you can tell me? You see any strange characters here?"

"Here? Hell, Crome. They're all strange characters."

Crome scanned the lot. In addition to his motorcycle, it contained a thirty-year-old rusted out pickup truck, an ancient Saab, and a banged-up Toyota. None of them resting on blocks. Crome had a hunch they all ran and were the vehicles of Dorman's wait staff.

"What I can't figure out is why?" Crome said. "And what they want. All I've got is this picture of her."

"Is the picture real?" Dorman asked.

"A guy I know who's good at that stuff is checking it out."

"You wanna beer or something?"

Crome looked around one more time. "You got any coffee?"

"Sure do."

Crome stopped at Maureen's trailer next. Since her son had joined the Navy and moved out, they had gone about christening every room in the most adventurous way. That is, when she wasn't pissed off at him for being a stubborn jackass.

Her son was out to sea and Crome had no idea how to contact him. He'd leave that alone until he knew more.

He used his key and went inside. Maureen didn't have much, but she took care of what she did have. Even when her son lived there, he had to keep his room and the bathroom squared away. Moving through the unit, Crome tried to think of what it usually looked like and if there was anything different. But he kept coming up short.

After walking through four times and getting more frustrated with each attempt, Crome sat down at the vintage metal kitchen table to think.

Maureen was a smart woman. Life had dealt her a tough hand. She'd managed to make the most of it. If she had been taken against her will here, she'd have left clues.

He got up and went outside. The short, gravel drive was empty.

Where was her car? It wasn't at the bar and it wasn't here.

The nine-acre island Blu called home was surrounded by marsh and changed in size depending on the tide. His great grandfather had bought the land for next to nothing and built a life on it. Each generation of Carraway men had married and produced a son. Blu was the first to challenge the tradition—he was divorced and so far had no son. Well, really he was the second. His father had broken the tradition by going out and marrying a Cuban woman. Blu's mother had escaped Castro's Cuba as a child and had made her way with her family to Miami on a flimsy boat. Blu's father met her there, they'd fallen in love, and he brought her to Charleston. They traveled now, living off a small inheritance from her father.

A small herd of wild horses called Carolina Marsh Tackeys, a breed indigenous to the lowcountry, had come with the island and never left even though there was no fencing. Blu filled the water trough for the horses with a garden hose and watched his daughter park her ancient Suzuki Sidekick beside his truck. She'd taken care of things at his house while he was out of town.

Hope's twenty-one-year-old smiling face beamed at him and his heart lifted.

She got out of her vehicle. "Hi, Dad."

The less intelligent of the Tackeys, a pair named Dink and Doofus, left the trough and blocked her path. From a survival standpoint, these two wouldn't stand a chance. The fight-or-flight instinct had not developed in them. On the other hand, intelligence could be measured many ways. They stood guard to collect the entrance fee—treats. Dink's brown mane had a few new tangles in it. Doofus' dirty snow coat looked cleaner, most likely due to an earlier gallop through the surf.

The temperature crested ninety-five, causing Blu to wipe sweat off his face.

Hope gave each horse an apple and came over and hugged her father. "How're you doing?"

It wasn't just a surface question. Hope wanted to know about Billie.

"I'm okay," he said.

After eyeing him for a minute—she was his daughter, after all, and therefore inclined to investigate—she let it go. "How's Mick?"

Blu had called her from the private jet on his return from Belize and told her about the kidnapping and to be careful.

"Tougher question," he said. "Holding it together, but he's wound up real tight."

So tight that since Blu returned from the security detail, he hadn't seen his partner take a drink.

While the horses chomped on their treats, Hope retrieved a satchel from her truck. The Latin skin she'd inherited from Blu gleamed in the sunlight. With her long, curly hair, high cheekbones, and button nose, she was eye-catching and, to Blu, beautiful as only a daughter could be to her father.

She held the bag up. "I brought sub sandwiches. Want to eat on the back porch?"

"Sure."

They set up on the porch underneath a spinning ceiling fan. Blu had refrained from installing air conditioning in his house, although his tolerance to the heat waned as the years ticked on. While the mosquitoes ignored Blu, they devoured everyone else. Hope sprayed on a layer of bug repellant before she sat.

Unwrapping a sub, she asked, "How can I help you and Mick find Maureen?"

"I don't want you to help at all," Blu said and realized he shouldn't have.

"With all due respect, Dad, I didn't ask if I could help. I asked how I could help. The difference is subtle but I figured you'd pick up on it." Hope had her mother's beauty. From him, she'd gotten her eyes and skin. And also her doggedness. Sometimes it was like arguing with himself, and how could one do that?

Not very well, as he'd found out over the years.

"I'm sorry it came out that way," he said. "You know it's not that I don't think you could, it's that—"

"It's that you're afraid something will happen to me. I get it."

"You say you get it. And I think you do on some level. But..." He paused and gathered his thoughts. "It was like last year when Harmony and Tess helped me and Mick. They were smart and driven. But I lost sleep over worrying about them and they aren't even my flesh and blood. I'm asking you, for my sake, to stay on the sidelines. If I put you in any danger again...let's just say I don't want to."

The sound of a second car pulling to a stop on the crushed-shell drive saved him from saying something else that wouldn't make sense to anyone who wasn't a father.

Peering around the corner, he saw Detective Roger Powers get out of an unmarked Charger with dark tinted windows. The car had a big motor and Blu thought more than once about picking up one from auction to have for tailing and chasing. He waved at his friend.

Powers wore a loose polo over jeans, the shirt partially hiding a police-issue Glock clipped to his belt. Around Blu's age with his hair graying at the temples, he walked with a confident gait.

His middle-age paunch still in its infancy, Powers said, "Sorry to interrupt y'all's lunch."

"No worries," Blu said. "Hope brought enough for four. You want a sandwich?"

"Sure," he said, "as long as you got something other than cold coffee or tap water to wash it down."

Hope held up a partial six-pack of Blenheim root beer.

Powers actually smiled. "She's a good planner. You should hire her."

Of all the damn things he could say.

"That's what I've been trying to tell him," Hope said.

"I don't have any open positions." Blu met her gaze. "Especially for relatives."

Powers doused himself in bug repellant and pulled out an empty chair. "This place could use a woman's touch. I think you should reconsider."

"No."

But Powers didn't let up. "Have her work here. Or, better yet, get an actual office. Someplace closer to, say, civilization. She could man the phone, do your invoicing. You know, the administrative stuff."

"Wait a minute," Hope said. "I want to be in the field."

Both men said, "No!"

To Powers, she said, "I thought you were on my side."

"I am," he said. "But the crap your old man and his renegade partner pull rides the ragged edge of legality. And sanity."

"But—"

Another simultaneous, "No!"

Hope backed her chair up from the table, stood, grabbed her purse, and stomped off in her new pair of espadrilles, the sandals she'd wanted for her birthday—the only reason he knew what to call them. Without looking back, she got in her SUV and left.

Blu watched her go.

Powers said, "Sorry about that."

After the sound of her tires on the crushed-shell drive trailed off, Blu said, "Don't be." He thought for a moment and looked at Powers. "And I actually think your suggestion makes sense. At least the part about her helping out around here."

Powers picked up one of the sub sandwiches, unwrapped an end, and took a bite. With a loaded mouth, he said, "Sub Station II. Good stuff. You should definitely hire her."

Chapter Five

Blu drove into Charleston and parked at the offices of the Palmetto Pulse, the place where Harmony and Tess used to work. Their former boss, Patricia Voyels, owned one of three remaining local news organizations in the city. The rest had fallen on hard times thanks to the industrial-powered vacuum social media had created. Now, anyone and everyone could report the news.

Patricia's great niece, Josie, worked part-time while attending the College of Charleston. The woman who'd previously worked the front desk, Ms. Dell, had taken a buyout from Patricia in anticipation of the sale of the business and moved to Orangeburg to care for an elderly family member. Patricia had said Josie was a crackerjack researcher with a knack for getting around password protected sites.

Destined for a life of crime, Blu thought. He'd keep her in mind for future jobs if she was interested in some extra under-the-table money.

Josie said, "Hey, Mr. Carraway. I'll let her know you're here."

As she picked up the phone, Patricia, beautiful and timeless as always, walked into the reception area. She had on her usual attire of a silk blouse of some kind, a skirt that ended an inch above her knees, and expensive-looking heels. Her dark hair had gray in it, but was thick and complimented her brown eyes.

He followed her back to her office and took a seat in a visitor's chair. She sat at her antique desk facing a pair of computer screens.

Word on the street was the bids for her empire had climbed into eight figures. For someone who'd started with nothing and cut her teeth in Southeast Asia covering underground U.S. operatives in Vietnam, she'd come a long way. Hard work and determination had paid off.

She rotated in her seat to face Blu and gave him a smile. "My nephew thinks of you like an older brother. It took a while, but I think he now exercises good judgment most of the time. As long as he stays off my headlines."

Blu had to smile at that one. It was Brack who'd given her news organization quite a renaissance when Patricia headlined his antics while tracking her ex-husband's killer.

"He saved my daughter," Blu said. "That's good enough for me."

Patricia's grin widened. "One of his finer moments."

The truth was Patricia's organization did not carry the clout it once had. Her star news correspondent, Darcy Wells, became Darcy Pelton when she married Brack. Harmony's and Tess' recent departure left Patricia with a significant void in the headline-reporting arena.

"So what can I do for you?" she asked. "You don't normally come around just to chat."

"Someone took Crome's girlfriend."

The smile left Patricia's face. "What?"

"We don't have much to go on. I think the goal is to mess with him. They sent a picture of her with a gun to her head."

"My God."

"Harmony and Tess are on it," Blu said. "And they've already been in contact with Darcy."

"What can I do to help?"

"I'm not sure, yet," Blu said. "I have a feeling this isn't just some vendetta. No one who knows him would arbitrarily pick a fight with Mick Crome. They'd have to want to die a painful death, be crazy, or be something worse."

Patricia made a few notes on a pad. "I'll get my staff on it right now."

Blu stood. "Thanks."

She looked at him. "How's Billie?"

Through a tight smile, he said, "She's good," and walked out.

Mick Crome sipped coffee from a paper cup outside a Starbucks while leaning against his motorcycle. The triple shot elixir wasn't Benzedrine, but it did the trick. He'd sworn off the red pills and nothing was going to send him back to them, but he still needed the rush. With his heart rate already jacked from the caffeine, he increased the nicotine level in his vape pen to the point of seeing imaginary pink elephants.

His mind raced through photographs of all the jokers from his past. He narrowed the list of enemies down to around thirty by ranking how bad he'd left them. The only problem with this logic was its reliance on a linear scale of pain and suffering.

He finished the coffee, crushed the cup, and tossed it into a receptacle.

A plan formed in his mind. He'd keep Blu busy. Same with the blonde twins. This was his problem to deal with. He didn't need or want them getting in the way. Or maybe being charged with murder along with him.

The old building in front of Crome would fail the current fire code. Exit doors were supposed to swing out. This one didn't, which made it easy for him to raise his foot and use all the strength in his leg to kick the door in.

The look on Phineous' face when his door got kicked in was, to Crome, one of horror—exactly what the biker was going for.

Crome said, "My partner dropped off a jump drive with a picture on it for you to look at. I want to know right now what you've got. And don't shuck me or so help me God I'll break your neck."

Phineous backed away, his hands up in surrender. The poor guy might have even pissed his pants.

Crome said, "I'm waiting."

"Wha-wha-what?"

"Don't give me that." Crome shoved a chair into the wall as he walked the narrow corridor of the makeshift office. "And don't even think about angling to get Harmony and Tess over here. For anything."

Phineous moved his head up and down like a jackhammer. "Okay, okay, okay."

"Good." Crome leaned against a table. "Now tell me what you know."

"Bl-Blu was coming back in a few hours."

Crome slammed his fist on the table. "Dammit! I'm here now."

The lanky photo analyst stumbled into a rack, sending various optical instruments crashing to the floor. They'd looked expensive.

"One more time, Phin," Crome said. "What have you got?"

"I might've found something in the pic."

"No kidding?" Crome gave him a genuine smile. "Knew you could do it, kid."

Phineous took a deep breath. "It's over there on the drafting table."

"Really?" Crome said, all harshness gone. "Right over there? Well, let's have us a look. Whaddaya say?"

Nodding, Phineous gestured toward the table.

Crome walked over and centered himself over the photograph of Maureen with her scared eyes looking directly at the person who had her.

Tuesday

The man ran his fingers through Maureen's long, brown hair, twirling the ends before releasing the strands and starting again. Its softness was intoxicating.

Someone as strong-willed as Maureen would not crack easily. Except maybe under the right circumstances. And really, that was all that interested him—the right circumstances. She was just a pawn in the chess match he'd begun with Crome. He'd selected white and made the first move this time.

The move from the hotel room to their current location was necessary. He had better control of her here. The hotel itself had been a needed challenge. He wasn't sure he could control her and needed a location that couldn't be linked to him in case things went south at the beginning. Now that he had her under control—drugged—he was able to make the move. Looking back, he realized he had overplanned. But, it was better to over plan than get caught short.

She worked hard for the meager money she made. Maureen stared at herself in the mirror he'd placed in front of her. Her skin, a tan hue that only the sun could create, was beautiful. She'd aged better than most women. In his opinion, it was because of her hard work. Slouching around brought on death and disease. But work was good for one's soul. He truly believed that, and Maureen proved it.

The only negative was her choice to blemish her flesh with ink. Tattoos betrayed natural beauty. But even with them, Maureen was a stunning woman. And now she was his. He'd taken her but she wasn't the prize. Crome's desperation to get her back was. It was the same with his partner, Blu Carraway. Both men deserved what was about to come their way.

Finding those right circumstances to make Maureen crack would be a bonus.

It didn't help that Paco had failed. He'd hoped to keep Blu away from Charleston and busy or dead in Belize. Now, he'd have to deal with both men together. Doable, but not preferable.

Chapter Six

Blu drove into North Charleston, parked in front of Phineous' run down shop, and knew that something wasn't right.

Phineous was a creature of habit. He could always be found either at his apartment getting stoned or at his office working. He had his groceries and food delivered, cut his own hair, and never went on vacation.

The closed sign on the front door said quite a bit. Blu had never seen it there, even after hours. Phineous was always diligent in locking his doors, but any signage was lacking. He didn't need to advertise.

Blu got out of his SUV and checked the door to the office—locked. He turned around and looked up and down the sidewalk. The area was desolate, a detail someone like Phineous probably enjoyed. Blu peered through the dirty window into the shop. The place was never clean, but Blu saw broken equipment on the floor, as if it had fallen.

He turned around, a nagging feeling that something wasn't right.

And then it hit him. What bothered him about the situation— Crome.

His partner would have gone in, scared Phineous to death, got whatever the analyst had, and then told him to get out of town or he'd kill him.

In his current frame of mind, Crome wouldn't care about burning bridges. This trait probably contributed to why Maureen was taken.

Blu walked back to his Nissan, got in and turned the air on. It had been a blessing that some idiots shot up his old truck, forcing him to get a newer one—one with working AC.

With cool air blowing, Blu called Crome. Of course it went to voicemail.

Crome checked his phone and saw it was "BLUE" calling. His partner's previous client had given him the phone and saddled him with a number that spelled out the color.

He let the call go to voicemail. There was no sense dealing with that reality just yet—the one that would tell him he needed to get himself under control. The one that had good intentions and only wanted to help. Well, by God, he didn't want any help. Not since Phineous had told him what he needed to know.

In fact, Blu was probably at Phin's shop right now, looking at the mess and realizing Crome had hijacked the lead. That put Crome thirty minutes ahead of him. Actually, a lot more than that because Blu would have to track down Phineous which would take a few hours, even for somebody as good as his partner. Not that he stashed him someplace inconspicuous. It was more like hiding him in plain sight.

Crome took a hit off his vape pen, exhaled, hot-boxed another drag right on top of the first, and then put it in his pocket. The double shot from the nicotine-laced vape juice coursed through his veins and cleared his head.

His target was directly ahead of him. Phineous had told him what he'd found in the picture, or rather in the reflection from Maureen's iris. Jesus, the camera imaging was good these days. The photo analyst had been able to zoom in something like five times and print out an image.

The photograph he'd been sent of Maureen with the gun to her head was really a reflection off a mirror. And it was cropped to show only her head and the hand holding the gun. But Phineous got a larger image from the reflection.

The picture showed the torso of the man who stood over Maureen and held the gun to her head with one hand and a smartphone with the other. His face was not in that image either, but more of the room was. Including things like a towel and a box of tissues. They told Crome the room was the bathroom. Another, smaller detail was also in the photo—the complimentary toiletries given at every hotel. Items like shampoo and conditioner and soap. Items that sometimes had the manufacturer's name printed on the packaging. Or, as in this case, the name of the hotel.

That was all Crome needed. It wasn't the top hotel in the city, but it was up there. The Palmetto Inn had a Meeting Street address and provided a short walk to the Market, one of Charleston's famous attractions.

Even in his own head, that sounded like some travel agent BS, but he gave himself a break. Caffeine and nicotine ingested at levels large enough to drop cattle did have a few side effects.

Blu had to track down Phineous, and fast. He had a hunch, a real bad one, that Crome had gotten to the poor guy first and scared him. While Blu agreed with the sense of urgency, he also believed in being pragmatic. He hoped he could smooth things over with Phineous when he found him.

He called Gladys. Gladys was a DMV contact who helped him pro bono after he got her out of an abusive marriage. She verified Phineous' last known address which was not too far from his shop, and he made his way there.

"There" turned out to be an old but decent apartment complex Blu had visited previously for other photo jobs. The brick buildings were still coated with green mildew, and pine trees and worn-out cars were scattered throughout the lot.

Blu parked, got out of his vehicle, and knocked on the second-floor door.

There was no answer.

He called out, "Phineous?"

Again there was no answer.

"Come on Phineous. It's Blu."

Still no answer.

The other detail Gladys had confirmed was the type of vehicle Phineous drove—a ten-year-old Prius.

There were no Priuses in the lot.

Aside from the office and here, where else could he look?

Blu pulled his iPhone out and made another call.

Tess Ray answered on the second ring with, "You find Crome?"

"No." Apparently she had more faith in him than he'd put in himself.

"Okay, what do you need?"

He said, "I think Crome scared Phineous enough that the poor guy left town. We need to track him down."

"Yessir," she said, but not convincingly.

"I'm serious," he said. "I think my partner just burned an important bridge and I need to fix it and find Crome before he does something else this stupid."

"He's only trying to find Maureen."

"I understand that, but he's trying to do it alone and I'm not going to let him."

"Seems you don't have a choice at the moment."

"Sure I do," he said. "Find me Phineous."

After a moment of silence, she said, "I will do what I can, but we need to talk about your bedside manner."

"This is my friend," he said, realizing he'd been testy with Tess just now. "I'm sorry. Any help you can give would be appreciated."

"Was that so difficult?" she asked.

Crome scoped out the hotel lobby trying to get a read on the place: white tile-floors, gray marble wainscoting and reception desk, high ceilings with brass chandeliers, and pretty people behind the counters.

Normally, he wasn't so conspicuous. But at this moment he

stood out as only a rough, tattooed biker in a sea of casually-dressed tourists could in an upscale hotel lobby.

He took a seat on one of the couches just off to the right and pulled out his phone and tried to become another clueless scroller while he formulated a plan.

What he needed was to figure out which room Maureen was in if she was even still here. Phineous hadn't been able to decipher much more out of the picture but the name of the hotel on the toiletries. Crome needed a friendly face he could drag into this mess.

None of the pretty people serving the guests had friendly faces. They all had pleasant but professional faces without blemishes. And they'd call the police.

Then he remembered that Blu had befriended a Latina woman who cleaned rooms in one of the other hotels. She'd helped him out by searching a room for him after the guests had checked out and found a tube of lipstick they'd later linked to a victim by the fingerprints still on it. Since then, she'd been brought into the Blu Carraway Investigations fold as a contractor and Crome had made sure to introduce himself to her.

Realizing that since he couldn't identify the kidnapper but the kidnapper could identify him, Crome got up and left. He found Juanita's number in his phone as he walked out and gave her a call.

"*Buenos días, señorita,*" he said.

"*Hola,* Mr. Crome."

Just like Gladys and her access to the limitless DMV database, Juanita Moralles, the hotel housekeeper, could provide a unique service.

In Spanish he said, "Do you know anyone who works at The Palmetto Inn?"

After a pause, in Spanish, she replied, "I think so. Let me make a call. What do you need?"

"I've got a picture that I think was taken in one of the rooms there but I want to see if they can narrow my search a bit."

"I'll see what I can do. Give me a few hours."

He didn't really have a few hours, but wasn't about to push the housekeeper like he did Phineous. He could rebuild that bridge by hooking the poor sap up with loose women. If he pushed Juanita the wrong way, she'd clam up and make sure neither he nor Blu could get any information out of her or any of her friends in the Latin community—a really bad idea.

He walked to a local restaurant, sat at a table, and ordered lunch. America was great for a lot of reasons—one of them being that no one really knew how much money anyone else had. Guys driving Bentleys couldn't afford to fill up their gas tanks. The little old lady in the rusted-out Chevy had ten million in gold. And a biker with worn jeans and a scruffy leather vest like himself could be sitting on several hundred thousand dollars in the Caymans that no one else, including the U.S. government, knew about.

He drank black coffee at a local watering hole and thought about Maureen and how scared she must be. It was how he kept his edge. He couldn't afford to let himself relax until she was safe and her kidnapper was dead.

Juanita called Crome within the hour. She did have a friend who worked there. And she started her shift at five.

Chapter Seven

Blu's phone chirped while he trolled the streets of Charleston looking for Crome's bike. He pulled over to the curb in an open parking spot by a meter, mentally kicking himself for not sneaking a LoJack tracker on his partner's modified Harley. He checked his texts and found a message from Tess.

It read, *Phin is at the Pirate's Cove.*

Why in the hell would the geek be there, unless Crome set him up with an unlimited tab or something.

At the moment, the reason wasn't as important as getting to the Isle of Palms as soon as possible. He sent a "thanks" text to Tess, put his truck in gear, and accelerated away.

Juanita's friend met Crome in the parking lot of the Charleston Visitor's Center located at the intersection of Meeting and Ann Streets. Her name was Fabiana. Juanita had said Fabiana was a single mother working to provide for her family. Crome took that to mean she expected him to pay her friend for any information she provided.

With about a grand in cash on him, he leaned on his bike in a parking spot and waited. A fifteen-year-old Dodge Neon pulled to a stop in the spot beside him. A Latina woman Crome would peg at a hard-working thirty got out. She wore the uniform of someone who performed housekeeping duties in any number of hotels.

When he straightened up, he realized he was a good foot taller than this woman. To not intimidate her like he did Phineous, he said, in Spanish, "I'm Mick Crome. Are you Juanita's friend, Fabiana?" It helped to have the U.S. Army teach him the language and a bi-lingual business partner to keep the skill up.

She looked him over, probably judging the biker boots, worn jeans, weathered leather vest, mustache and week-old beard, aviator shades, and long hair sticking out below a do-rag that was his usual attire. After a moment, she said, "*Si.*"

"Can you look at a picture and see if you can tell me which room it could be?"

She nodded.

He said, "I have to warn you. It is not a pleasant picture. But I could really use your help to find the woman in it."

Her eyes were big and brown and the lines around them showed a lot of tough years. He got the sense that she had already seen more in this life than many ever would. She said, "I understand."

Crome slid a folded piece of paper out from the inside pocket of his vest. It was a copy of the picture the sick son-of-a-bitch with a death wish had sent him. Crome unfolded it and handed it to her.

Fabiana looked at the picture of Maureen with her scared eyes and the pistol aimed at her head, blinked, and put her free hand to her mouth.

He waited for her to get past the shock and look at the surrounding details. The speed at which she adjusted would tell him how much violence she'd seen in her short life—his guess was a lot.

That profile of her was confirmed when the surprise in her eyes quickly turned to focus as she analyzed the fringes of the photo.

"I'm sorry for this woman," Fabiana said. "I understand now and want to help her as best I can."

Crome said, "*Gracias.*"

"You found out which hotel it was by the bottles of shampoo and conditioner."

"*Si.*"

She looked up from the picture. "Most of the rooms in the hotel are similar. One difference is that they can be exact opposites of each other. Like right-handed or left-handed."

He nodded. "Can you tell that from the picture?"

"No," she said. "The bathrooms are arranged the same."

"Damn."

"But this isn't one of our regular rooms. This is a suite. I can tell by the bathtub and shower in the background."

"How many suites you got there?"

"Twenty."

She'd just narrowed his search from several hundred rooms to twenty. He had to refrain from picking Fabiana up and kissing her.

She asked, "Does that help you?"

In as calm a voice as he could muster, given this new intel, he said, "It does. Any chance I can get the names of the guests who stayed in those rooms over the last week?"

"They don't give me that information."

What he understood her to mean was that she didn't have access to it. He pulled out a fold of hundred-dollar bills and handed her three of them. "This is for what you've given me. If you can get me a list of who the guests were, I'll give you the rest of it." He held the fold up for her to see. "And if you can get it to me tonight, I'll double it."

"Juanita told me you were an honorable but hard man," she said, her dark eyes staring into his. "I believe her. But I have two children to take care of. That is a lot of money but it won't be enough if I lose my job."

Deflated, he said, "I understand."

She gave him a look, one filled with pity and empathy. "I'll see what I can do."

He again had to restrain himself from kissing the woman.

Blu found Phineous sitting at one of the tables inside the Pirate's Cove bar. With him were two women of questionable morals.

Strippers, if Blu had to guess. In fact, he didn't have to guess. When Crome wasn't spending time with Maureen or Tess and Harmony, he could be found in the presence of such acquaintances. And these were two of his favorites.

As he walked up to the table behind Phineous, Blu struggled to keep his eyes on their faces and off their cleavage.

The women, artificial blondes the both of them, said, "Hey Blu!"

Mid-thirties, they'd seen more than their fair share of degenerate men and had done more than their fair share of white powder and other chemicals. Yet, somehow they'd survived the life this long.

Blu said, "Hey Krystal. Hey Amber," using their stage names, the only names he knew them by.

Phineous turned around, saw Blu, and started to get up as if to bolt.

Blu gently but firmly pushed him back into his seat. "Don't get up on my account, Phineous."

"I-I was—"

"Save it."

So Crome had scared the bejesus out of Phineous and then compensated him with a fun-filled evening consisting of Krystal and Amber. For a guy like Phineous, there were always worse things that could happen. But there were probably fewer chances for something better. Phineous looked like a wet pack of noodles with his pale skin and thin neck, arms and legs.

Blu slid the empty chair out and sat facing Phineous. "Your shop was closed when I came by. I thought you were working on the photo for me."

Phineous' cheeks reddened. "I gave what I had to Crome. He's your partner, isn't he?"

It sounded to Blu like Phineous actually had a backbone, even if his torso said otherwise. Blu said, "Why don't you give what you have to me?"

Phineous sighed. "Samples of shampoo on the sink counter

were from The Palmetto Inn."

"Thank you."

Krystal said, "Oh. I've never stayed there. Why don't the four of us get a room?"

Before anyone else could reply, Blu leaned over to her.

She let him kiss her cheek.

"Maybe some other time," Blu said. "But I've got to get to work. I'm sure Phineous'll get a room for you all."

Krystal dropped her chin in an exaggerated form of disappointment. But the truth was Crome probably already paid her and Amber well for this job. And Phineous, if he didn't have any bad habits Blu didn't know about, most likely had quite a bit of money squirreled away. He could afford a nice room for the three of them to close out the evening.

Blu got up from the chair and found Brack Pelton, the owner of the Pirate's Cove, in his office. Pelton looked up from the desk where he was reading some papers when Blu rapped on the door. Shelby, Pelton's dog, had been sleeping on the couch and jumped up ready to attack until he realized he knew Blu already.

Instead, the dog leapt off the couch and ran up to him.

Blu knelt and greeted Shelby with a pat on the head and a long scratch behind his ears. "How's it going?

"I'm thinking of taking up drinking again," Pelton said, with a smile.

"That good, huh?"

Leaning back in his chair, he said, "It's better than you look."

Blu didn't reply.

"Crome was here when he got the voicemail from Maureen." He then pointed to the dining area. "And he set up your photo guy with the strippers out there."

"Sorry about that."

"Looks to me like Crome did him a favor."

"I'm glad you think so," Blu said. "Someone else might not appreciate the gesture."

"They're attracting all the Yankee husbands in the vicinity.

And all of them are spending an awful lot of money in my bar while they gape."

Blu nodded.

Pelton asked, "How can I help?"

One of the reasons Blu liked his job was the periodic action it provided. His Army Ranger days were over, but any combat was like blood to a canine. Once they had the taste, they always wanted more of it. Blu wanted the action, needed the action.

And Pelton had gotten the same taste in Afghanistan. He was ten years younger than Blu and Crome, and a Marine, but he'd chewed similar sand and tasted the same blood.

Chapter Eight

From his truck while still parked in the Pirate's Cove parking lot, Blu called Patricia Voyels, Pelton's aunt, and asked her about the hotel.

She said, "What would you or my nephew do without me?"

Blu laughed. "I guess we'd have to find real jobs."

"Truer words were never spoken," she said. "I know the Palmetto Inn owner. He owes me a favor. And tell Harmony and Tess that I want the exclusive on this. They owe me, too." She ended the call.

He walked back inside the bar to Pelton's office. Pelton was still at his messy desk. Shelby came up to Blu again.

Blu petted the fifty pound lady killer. "Your aunt is cashing in her chips, isn't she?"

Pelton sat back in his seat again. "Why do you ask?"

"She's been nothing but helpful to me since I met her. But now she seems even more so."

Pelton reclined and put his hands behind his head. "Don't forget she's got a crush on you."

"She needs someone a little more mature than me," Blu said. "And I'm not trying to crack an age joke here."

"Don't I know it. I've got twenty-year-old waitresses more mature than either of us. So's my dog."

From behind Blu, a female voice said, "He's the reason we're still in business."

It was Paige, Pelton's business manager.

Blu said, "Ah, the brains of the operation."

"Don't forget looks too. Next to Shelby, of course."

She wasn't kidding, either. Long, brown hair with sun-bleached highlights, tanned skin, and a personal trainer figure, Paige was tough. About ten years older than Blu's daughter and married with a son. None of that stopped Crome from taking a run at her, except that she shut him down with a smile and a pat on the head.

Blu's phone buzzed in his pocket and he excused himself from the room.

It was Patricia and he answered.

"The owner wasn't real happy about the picture," She said. "I told him we'd do everything we could to keep it out of the media, but it required him to stretch a few of the hotel policies."

"Did he bite?"

"He's a good business man," she said. "It's usually not a hard decision if the choice is a nuclear explosion or an air raid. He went with the air raid."

"Meaning he'll play ball on the list of guests?"

"Affirmative. In fact, I've already got it in front of me. Most of the rooms have turned over since yesterday. All of them have been cleaned and none of the women who clean the rooms reported seeing anything suspicious."

"Okay. I'm on my way to you."

With more than a hint of something not quite business-oriented in her voice, she said, "I was hoping you'd say that."

He ended the call, in awe at the expression of true power she'd just wielded. Blu had a carte blanche connection in Adam Kincaid, Jennifer's father, because he'd once had to go to Mexico to rescue the man's daughter. But he never abused it. With one phone call, Patricia got him something he would have had to work days to get, maybe even have Josie hack into the hotel database if his own sleuthing didn't do the trick.

*   *   *

Tuesday evening

Fabiana came through again for Crome. He now held in his hands several sheets of paper—copies of the housekeeping log from The Palmetto Inn. The names of the guests were printed along with each room. She had provided him with everyone from the last week.

The first thing he noticed was that the rooms had all changed occupants, meaning Maureen wasn't there anymore.

Sitting in a McDonald's in Mount Pleasant, his favorite type of coffee house—one that served an inexpensive yet good cup of Joe along with all the food he could want—Crome held one of the sheets of paper with his right hand while his left hand kept his mouth busy with a Big Mac.

None of the names rang a bell. He'd have to run down each one of them, and he didn't have time to do that.

His phone buzzed. He looked at the display, saw Harmony's name, and answered.

She said, "What the hell, Crome?"

"Howdy to you, too."

"You scare Phineous half to death and then bribe him with your hooker friends."

The volume of his phone was such that everyone around him in the restaurant could hear her, and it was about half full of people at the time.

"They were strippers, not hookers."

"Strippers dance around poles and take their clothes off in a club. The two ladies you hired got him drunk and took him to a hotel room."

Crome didn't have a quick response to that one. He just hoped Phineous had protection.

"What was that?" she asked. "No snappy comeback? I didn't think so."

"Are you going to help me or are you going to run your

mouth?"

Apparently it was her turn to be quiet.

He really didn't have the patience for this. He needed to find Maureen. Why couldn't Harmony or Blu or Phineous or who-the-hell-ever see what was at stake?

"You know," Harmony said, "if it weren't Maureen's life on the line, I really wouldn't give a flip what happened to you. But she's an innocent. And frankly she deserves a medal for putting up with you. So, to answer your question, I'm going to help you, and I'm going to run my mouth. And if you're not careful, I'm going to bring those two body builders Blu works out with and let them pinch your sorry head off your sorry neck and stick it on a post in my front yard."

"Jesus," Crome said.

"No," she said. "My name is Harmony, and I make good on my threats."

The call went dead in his ear.

He put the phone down and looked around. Everyone in the place snuck sideways glances at him. Normally, he was the baddest badass in the room. Today was not a normal day.

Today, he had just been bitch-slapped by a co-ed.

His phone buzzed again. Crome looked at it and saw Blu's number. Since he didn't feel like getting another lecture, he let it run to voicemail.

As he waited for the buzzing to stop, a glint of reflection from the parking lot caught his attention. He looked out the window and saw his partner standing beside his motorcycle. And he didn't look happy.

Chapter Nine

Folly Beach, Charleston County, Saturday, October 2000

Hope sat on a plastic adult chair, giggled, and said, "Daddy!"

Children ran around the backyard, playing tag.

Blu snapped the photo, catching his daughter looking directly into the camera with a big smile on her young face. A coned birthday hat with the words "I'm 3 today!" was on her head and she held a bright-colored pinwheel.

"Did you get the picture?" asked Abby.

Hope's mother and Blu's wife, Abby, had long, brown hair, blue eyes, and, a tall, slender physique. Thank God Hope had gotten her mother's looks. She also had Blu's eyes and Latin skin tone. It made for an irresistible combination in the little girl. Blu would be in trouble when boys weren't icky any more.

Abby was just playing nice for Hope's day. Things weren't going well for them in marriage-land.

Filled with pride in the beauty and innocence of Hope, Blu said, "Yeah, I think so."

Abby went over to Hope, lifted her off the chair, and placed her on her feet in the grass. "Go play with your friends, sweetie."

Hope giggled again and ran to the group of children, making sure to hold the pinwheel up so that it spun when the air rushed around it.

Blu said, "You've done a nice job with this today."

"No thanks to you," she said.

It was a true statement on the surface. He hadn't offered any direct help in the planning. But he'd made sure there was money set aside for it, even working extra hours moonlighting as a bouncer in a few clubs when nothing else was paying off. He didn't reply because it wouldn't help anything.

The chugga chugga of a Harley could be heard coming down the street.

Abby said, "Sounds like Mick."

The engine rumble got louder, revved one last time, and then went silent. A moment later, a tall, lanky man with long brown hair held back with a bandanna, aviator sunglasses and handlebar mustache strode around the side of the house carrying a decent-sized teddy bear with a bow tied around its neck.

Hope saw the man about the same time Abby and Blu did. "Uncle Mick!"

She ran to him and jumped into his open arm.

Crome held Hope up in one arm and the teddy bear in the other.

Blu aimed the camera and snapped a picture of his business partner holding his daughter.

Abby joined Hope and Crome.

Blu took a few more photos and then watched the parents of the other children. They all worked normal jobs—bank tellers, machine operators, office managers, doctors and lawyers. Blu and Crome were the wild cards in this party—self-employed and free from most all of the constraints. Except for money.

Crome put Hope down. She turned and ran back to the other children with the teddy bear.

Abby said something to Blu's business partner and they both laughed.

At least she wasn't holding their marital problems against him.

Crome slid a pack of Winstons out of his jeans pocket, took one out, and lit up with a Zippo.

It surprised Blu when Abby motioned to a woman standing by the opened cooler with the beer to bring two bottles over to her and

Crome. Thanks to a case Blu had worked, the woman had gotten more than enough evidence against a cheating husband and was recently divorced. According to Abby, she was looking for a rebound and Blu guessed his wife was setting her up with Crome. He wondered if that was the best solution to the problem, Crome being Crome and all.

The man was always looking, and ran away from every commitment since he got out of the Army. Blu was surprised he'd agreed to join the business.

The woman, a cute redhead named Daron with a bob cut, freckles on her face and arms, and an outfit she most likely got from the Gap—white t-shirt, jean shorts, and flip flops, walked toward them. Her eyes were shielded behind shades but Blu knew they were green.

Daron approached Crome and Abby with both hesitation and a slight jitteriness. Any other time in her life, she wouldn't even consider Crome. But her husband had lived up to the cliché of leaving her, and their kids, for his secretary. This gave Crome the opportunity to be Crome and Daron the opportunity to show her husband up.

Abby left Daron with Crome and came up beside Blu.

"Why on God's green earth are you setting those two up?" Blu asked.

"Daron has always been the good wife," she said. "She got a raw deal. I told her about Crome and warned her not to try to attach any strings. She just wants someone to treat her nice. Crome can at least do that much."

"I hope you told him that."

Abby glared at him. "Of course I did. Anyone else, except you, I wouldn't have to say it."

"Where're her kids?" he said.

"At their grandparents'."

Hope ran up to them again. "Daddy, come push me on the swing."

Blu didn't know what he'd done to deserve Hope. She put

everything in perspective for him. He didn't matter. Abby didn't matter. Only Hope mattered. And that's what got him through the tough times.

Later on that day, Blu sat on a rocker on his front porch thinking. The phone rang in his home office and Abby answered. During off-hours, Blu had all calls routed from his downtown office.

Abby spoke in the professional tone she had trained herself to use.

He heard her say, "Please hold," and then she pressed the hold button which made a loud beep.

"Who is it?" he asked.

"A Mr. Ron Jansen from the Isle of Palms. He wants to meet you today."

Blu looked at his watch, a vintage Rolex his father bought off some local thieves in Vietnam who'd most likely pilfered the timepiece from some diplomat. His pawn shop connections already confirmed it was the real deal, vintage 1962. The hands said four o'clock.

Before he could say anything, Abby said, "You need the work."

She was right. In this business, it was either feast or famine. They'd learned not to blow all the money in the feast times because famine normally followed, like at present.

He took the receiver from her, pressed the button to take the call off hold, and said, "Mr. Jansen? This is Blu Carraway."

"Mr. Carraway," an even voice, not too high or low pitched, said, "I have a matter that I feel the need to seek professional advice on."

"If you want, I can refer you to several attorneys I work with."

Mr. Jansen said, "I don't need that kind of advice. Are you going to be in your office today? I know it's Saturday."

"I'll be glad to meet you. It can be there or anywhere else you'd like."

"Your office is fine. Six o'clock okay?"

"I'll see you then. Thanks for calling, Mr. Jansen."

The reply was a dial tone.

Blu had an instinct to call Crome but at the last minute thought better of it. Daron had ridden away with him on the back of his motorcycle and Blu didn't want to interrupt anything.

He kissed Hope goodbye.

Abby said, "I won't wait up."

Not knowing how to reply, Blu drove away in one of his work vehicles, an older Jeep Cherokee—the full-size model—his father had used. It sucked gas and had just rolled the odometer for the second time. Two hundred thousand miles on anything was respectable. Another vehicle of his, a seventy-two Dodge pickup, was equally tired and equally reliable. So were his two stake-out sedans. Abby got the newer vehicles, currently a slightly used Honda Accord they'd picked up as a lease turn in.

As the old Jeep lumbered across the bridges spanning the perpetual tidal creeks that made up the lowcountry of South Carolina, the setting sun glistened on the marsh grass as the shoots swayed in the wind. He punched in the cigarette lighter, stuck a Camel from a new pack in his mouth, and lit up when the lighter clicked back. Rolling with his left elbow resting out the open window—the air conditioning had gone out a while back and now consisted of four windows and sixty miles an hour—he held the Camel with two fingers and guided the wheel with the other three. He used his free hand to load a Misfits cassette into the deck, and when the punk band exploded out of his truck's speakers, it reminded him of the mosh pits of his misspent youth.

His two-room office overlooked King Street in downtown Charleston and included several parking spots behind the building which were currently empty. He parked and made his way up the back staircase. Sliding his key in the lock, he turned the knob and opened the door.

And found Crome with Daron.

On the couch against the wall.

Their clothes were scattered all over the floor.

Crome, lying on his back, said, "Howdy."

Daron, on top, turned fifty shades of red, grabbed a garment off the floor and tried to cover herself. It didn't exactly work.

Blu gritted his teeth for a few seconds, took a deep breath, and said, "We've got a client coming to meet me here any minute."

"Give us a moment, would ya?" Crome asked.

Blu backed out the way he came in, closed the door behind him, turned, and bumped into a smaller man with glasses and no hair on top but cut short on the sides. He was dressed in a nice polo shirt, khaki shorts, and leather sandals and had what looked like a natural tan. The man was fit enough, but not for fighting. Blu said, "Excuse me."

"Mr. Carraway?"

And the hits just kept coming.

Blu recognized the voice. He said, "Mr. Jansen?"

The man looked at Blu, at the closed door, and then back to Blu.

Blu held out a hand. "Sorry for my rudeness. It's nice to meet you."

Jansen shook his hand. "Do you mind if we go in?"

Thinking fast, Blu said, "My partner is interviewing another potential client. Do you mind if we take a walk instead?"

At that moment, the door opened and Daron exited, her face still red, followed by Crome who gave a nod to Blu and Jansen and said, "All yours."

Blu watched the couple walk down the steps to the first landing and turn the corner, the whole time trying not to think about how unprofessional their agency must appear. He held the door open for Jansen, who entered and stood in the reception area where the couch that Crome and Daron had just exercised sat.

The whole room smelled like sex—musky sweat and adrenaline.

Aside from the aforementioned couch, there were two desks in various degrees of neatness. Because the agency was small, the receptionist was Abby when she was available and an answering machine when she wasn't.

The office had the main room where the couch and desks were, a restroom, small kitchen area and a conference room.

Blu picked up a tablet and pen from his desk and led Jansen to the conference room, which had a decent-sized table and six chairs. For the money and location, he and Crome had lucked out. The current landlord had been a client who'd cut them a deal on rent after they'd cut him a deal on his case, a dead-beat tenant that needed to be evicted.

Blu asked, "Can I make some coffee for you?"

Jansen declined and took a seat.

Facing him, Blu said, "How can I help you, Mr. Jansen?"

The man fidgeted in his seat. "I think I'm being followed."

"By whom?" Learning Spanish from his mother had also helped his English.

"I'm not sure." Jansen looked him in the eye. "That's what I need you to find out."

"Do you want me to follow you to see who is following you?"

"Yes."

Easy enough. He and Crome had done similar jobs. He asked, "What do you want me to do if I find you're right and someone is following you?"

The fidgeting stopped. "I want you to blow their head off."

Blu thought Jansen was actually quite serious. "I'm sorry, Mr. Jansen. That's not really what we do here at this agency." It was as truthful of a statement as a politician's campaign promise.

"Okay," the smaller man said, "then what do you suggest?"

"We can identify the individual or individuals and perform a background check on them."

The fidgeting started up again. "Is that all?"

No, Blu thought. What he was thinking was that if this is for real and there is a threat, he and Crome could set the target up for a big fall. But he didn't want to suggest that just yet.

"We can offer you twenty-four-hour protection until we resolve the situation." It was a stretch. If it came to that, he and

Crome would have to hire an extra body or two. Even with Crome popping reds, he couldn't stay awake forever. At least, Blu didn't think so. But he didn't remember the last time he'd seen his partner sleep. The pills were a problem, but not a big enough one yet. At least not as big as the problems in Blu's marriage. He and his wife were passing ships in the night, sometimes on a collision course and sometimes in completely different oceans.

Jansen said, "I don't think that's going to solve my problem."

"Do you mind if I ask a direct question?"

The fidgeting stopped for the second time. "Okay."

"Is there anything that you're doing or are a part of that would attract people who wish to do you harm?"

He rubbed his fingers together, a different type of fidget.

It really didn't matter if Jansen answered the question honestly or not. Blu and Crome would soon figure this detail out whether the client wanted them to or not. What Blu wanted to know was whether Jansen would talk about it, be honest about it.

Jansen said, "I'm having an affair with a woman. A married woman."

"And you think her husband is after you?" What Blu was thinking was that Jansen might want the man out of the picture.

"Yes."

"Are you still in contact with the woman?"

"Yes."

"Casual or more serious?"

Sometimes, Blu felt like a priest hearing a confession. Clients, in laying their sins out on the table, still tried to sugarcoat the facts. If people could lie to God, they could lie to him.

Looking down at the table, Jansen said, "I love her."

Jansen was lying to him. Maybe not outright, but it was there. Blu felt it in his gut.

He said, "I'll need to know who the woman and her husband are."

Clenching his fists tight, Jansen said, "No one can know."

Again, Blu and Crome could find out fairly easily

Blu sat back. He felt like he'd reached a wall with this man. A wall that would come down sooner or later. It had to, especially if the woman's husband was some big shot with a big ego who didn't like a little man like Jansen slipping into his matrimonial bed. He said, "I think we can help you, Mr. Jansen. My partner and I run a small agency, but we get results."

For the first time since he'd met the man in person, Jansen smiled. "I heard that about you."

"Really?" Blu asked. "From whom?"

"Andeline."

Andeline. Madame Adeline, Queen of the Charleston elite escort service who provided discrete female companionship at top-shelf rates.

If Jansen spoke the truth about her, and one phone call would verify or contradict it, then the case was legit. If not, well, Blu could always look up the angry husband and offer to solve his problem for him. Blu would not let someone like Jansen falsely namedrop Andeline in the hopes of getting preferential treatment and get away with it. He had too much respect for the power she wielded and his own reputation for something like that.

And, Blu wondered how Jansen knew her. Most likely, it was from patronizing her business. So he'd moved from prostitutes to wives. Not exactly a safer avenue. One meant dodging all forms of sexually transmitted diseases. The other meant dodging angry, shotgun-wielding husbands.

Blu said, "If you want to retain the services of our investigation firm, the cost is four hundred down and four hundred a day plus expenses. Twenty-four-hour coverage is double."

The money didn't seem to phase this man.

While Blu retrieved a standard contract, Jansen presented a white bank envelope from his front pocket, opened the top flap, and pulled out a neat stack of hundred dollar bills. He counted out twelve, enough for the retainer and two eight-hour days. Handing them to Blu, he said, "This should be enough to get you started. I'll pay daily after that."

"Do you mind if I ask what you do for a living, Mr. Jansen?"

"I'm an economic advisor."

Blu noticed Jansen had a Cartier Tank watch. Even though he'd still verify the information, Blu felt comfortable that the man could afford to pay the freight. "I appreciate you considering our agency and I'll make sure to thank Andeline for the referral. Is there anything else you think I should know?"

Jansen said, "Just be careful and don't tip them off."

"Of course."

After Jansen signed the contract and left with his own copy, Blu locked up the office. They needed the job, even if it was only for a few days.

Chapter Ten

The next day, Sunday, lunchtime, October 2000

Blu sat at a table on the upper deck of the Pirate's Cove bar on the Isle of Palms and watched the surf while drinking a glass of sweet tea. The bar was a run-down two-story building in the distinctive shape of an old Spanish frigate with two decks that overlooked the Atlantic Ocean. While Blu preferred Folly Beach on the south side of Charleston, Crome had wanted to check this place out.

The rumor that the owner of the Pirate's Cove sold packs of smokes out of the vending machines with fake tax stamps sealed the deal.

"Ohio" by Crosby, Stills, Nash, and Young blared from an ancient jukebox.

Blu tapped his foot to the beat, thinking about the call to Andeline earlier.

She'd said, "I know Ron. He wants to run for office."

"Really?" Blu'd asked. "Is that why he thinks he's being followed?"

"I'm not sure," she'd said. "He only told me he needed someone tough to do some work for him. I, of course, thought of you and Mick."

"So he's one of your clients?" he'd asked.

"Now you know I have to keep confidences, right?"

"Well you have to know him from somewhere, And."

"You're right," she'd said. "Just like I know you from

somewhere."

One lousy night of weakness. Blu and Crome, fresh off the plane from war, pockets full of combat pay, wanting some companionship. Okay, maybe it wasn't so lousy. But he hadn't been back to Andeline's since, although he couldn't vouch for Crome. To top it off, once Blu had set up shop, she'd been really good about sending work his way.

"Okay," Blu'd said, "so the guy wants to be president. Anything else?"

"Powerful men sometimes have a thirst for things like women. And money."

"So this is about money?" He'd asked.

"I think so, but I'm not sure. There's some kind of important vote taking place."

Interrupting the memory, Crome pulled out an adjacent chair as Blu took a last drag from his Camel and stubbed it out in the ashtray on the table.

Before Blu could speak, Crome said, "Sorry about that earlier. I didn't know we had a client coming by."

"How long have you been using the office for your personal business?"

"Aw, come on, Blu," Crome said. "We had lunch at a deli on East Bay. Afterwards she wanted to see the place. One thing led to another and then you walked in."

Blu took a sip of his tea and swallowed. "I guess that's why your bike wasn't parked at the office. But you didn't exactly answer my question."

"You're right." Crome grinned. "Won't happen again."

"Pinky swear?" Blu held up his little finger.

"You serious?"

"Yep. Bonking Abby's friend in the office means you have to sit at this table and give me a pinky shake in front of all these people."

Crome shook his head. "This almost makes the whole thing not worth it."

"Really?" Blu had seen pretty much all of Daron, at least a lot more than he'd ever seen before. While it might be embarrassing for two tough guys like him and Crome to do some candy-ass thing like linking pinky fingers, he thought it was a small price to pay.

Crome grinned again. "You're right. She sure was pissed off at her ex. Wants me to come with her when she drops off the kids at his place later."

"Don't kill him," Blu said. It wasn't an out-of-line request if someone knew Crome. He could take things a tad far if pushed.

"I was thinking more along the lines of scaring the hell out of him."

Blu knocked two smokes out of his pack, handed one to Crome, and fired them both off from a book of matches that had the bar's flag—a cigar smoking jolly roger with a South Carolina state flag bandana and aviator sunglasses.

The bartender, a man in his fifties with long hair like Crome pulled back in a ponytail and wearing a faded Hawaiian shirt, asked them if they wanted lunch menus. He had a black patch over his right eye.

Crome said yes, but Blu wasn't sure he'd risk eating in the place. The ATF wasn't the only governmental agency the place was dodging. How it had managed to pass health code inspections would be an interesting mystery to solve.

Blu stuck with a tea refill and wondered if the eye-patch was a prop or actually covered an injury.

The CSNY song ended and "Along the Watchtower" by Hendrix began.

Crome ordered a burger, fries, and a draft beer, pulled a five off a fold of bills from his front pocket and handed it to the bartender. "This is for whoever is picking the tunes."

The bartender smiled and took the bill. "Thanks. That'd be me."

Crome nodded and the older man nodded back.

"You two ain't tourists," the older man said.

Blu and Crome would probably stand out in most places in Charleston. Both were big—over six-footers. Crome was the consummate biker. He wore do-rags, aviator sunglasses, week-old beards, leather vest jackets, worn jeans, and motorcycle boots.

Blu liked black—black t-shirt, black jeans, and black Doc Martens shoes. Tourists viewed them as oddities. Anyone on the job, living on the fringes of society, or previously incarcerated would recognize them as kindred spirits. Or enemies. Such was life in the gray area.

The bar's mascot, a beautiful red and blue macaw, sat on a perch next to the cash register. Without warning, it hopped up onto the bartender's shoulder.

Crome exhaled a cloud of smoke. "Nice bird."

The man stroked the bird's breast feathers. "This is Bonny."

The bird gave his ear a nibble and flew over a family of tourists seated at a table and landed on the railing at the far end of the deck. The old man went to serve another customer.

"You wanna hear about the job?" Blu asked his business partner.

"Looked like someone spooked the guy, you ask me," Crome said. "I'd say he pissed somebody off and now is worried about the blowback. If I hadda guess, I'd say he messed with someone else's woman."

Crome was a lot of things, but stupid and unobservant weren't on the list.

"That's most of it," Blu said. "The other part Andeline told me was the guy wants to enter politics. How would you handle it?"

"Andeline? No kidding. God love her. Did the man tell you who the chick-ee was?"

"No."

"Well, then," Crome said, "we know what we gotta do first."

After a few minutes with neither of them saying anything, the song changed to Eric Clapton and George Harrison playing "While My Guitar Gently Weeps."

The older man brought Crome's food order and sat the plate in front of him.

Crome said, "You really have a mean music collection."

The man took a pack of cigars out of his breast pocket, the plastic tipped kind, and stuck one between his lips.

Blu fired off another match from his book, one handed.

The man leaned forward and caught the end of his stogie on the flame. He straightened up and asked, "So who the hell are you guys?"

Crome hoisted his burger off the plate. "Abbott and Costello."

"No you're not," the man said, exhaling a cloud of smoke. "They're prettier than you lugs."

Blu said, "So we hear. You own this place?"

The man took the cigar out of his mouth, held it between two fingers, spread his arms and rotated from side to side. "Welcome to my humble abode."

Around a mouthful of burger, Crome said, "You live here, too?"

"It sure feels like it."

"Working for a living ain't what it's supposed to be, huh?" Blu asked. "Adam hosed us all in the garden when he didn't kill the snake before it got to Eve."

The man pointed at Blu with the two fingers holding the cigar. "A theologian and a soldier. The wonders never cease."

With a lot of self restraint, Blu asked, "What do you mean?"

Crome took a big gulp of beer. "Yeah. We look like soldiers to you?"

"I can smell military a mile away," the man said. "You guys ain't in it now, but you was. I'd stake my left eye on it."

Blu took a sip of his tea, set the glass back on the bar, and asked, "Is that patch for real or do you just wear it to get the girls?"

With a snort and a chuckle, the man said, "Good one. I deserved that. Yeah, it's real. Took a round from an AK over the rice patties."

He left them and went to serve another customer.

Blu said, "The old guy's somethin' else."

"Yeah," Crome said. "His name's Reggie Sails. I heard he flew planes for Air America in Vietnam. That story he told about his eye?

It's real. The guy took the hit and still landed the plane."

"No kidding?"

"Total badass."

Back to business, Blu said, "So you want dayshift or night?"

"You mean we gotta tail Poindexter?"

"Hey," Blu said, "it's your plan."

"Don't give me that shuck," Crome said. "You already had it worked out. Only now 'cause I said it, I own it. So fine, I'll take night. It'll give me more time on the office couch with Daron."

Blu turned and looked at his partner.

Crome grinned. "Got ya with that one, didn't I?"

"Since it's your plan and all," Blu said, ignoring his smug partner, "and since I sat on the guy's house last night, by the way, you can have tonight."

"I'm guessin' there wasn't much going on?"

"Stayed in all night," Blu said.

The older man returned, a glutton for punishment, obviously. Either that, or Blu and Crome were more interesting than the trickle of tourists spending part of their vacation money in his place.

Blu pulled his money fold out, ready to pay.

The man said, "Your money's no good here. Consider it a gift from one soldier to another."

Crome said, "That's awfully nice of you."

"Hell," the man said. "Just watchin' my other customers eyeball you two is worth at least your tab. Plus, it took their focus off me for a change. And that's saying something here."

Blu and Crome shook hands with Reggie, as he'd introduced himself, and walked out. On the sidewalk in front of the bar, they paused by Crome's Harley.

Crome said, "I'm going home to get some sleep. I get the feeling I'm gonna to need it. Poindexter looks like a real party animal."

He said it straight, but Blu caught the sarcasm.

Jansen might be the other man, but economic advisors, as he'd called himself, did not typically stay out all night closing down nightclubs. But some politicans led double lives. If Blu and Crome were lucky, Jansen might sneak out and meet his mistress.

Crome mounted his bike, gave Blu a salute, started the V-twin engine, and roared off.

Blu watched his friend head up Ocean Boulevard toward the connector that tied the north end of Mount Pleasant to the island. Then he decided that since he was there, he'd take a walk on the beach. So that's what he did.

Chapter Eleven

October 2000

Blu Carraway Investigations had two cars they used specifically for tailing people and both were popular, midsized sedans sold by the hundreds of thousands every year. Invisible would be how Crome described them. They weren't fast, but they had working air conditioning and started every time, unlike his partner's SUV.

After sitting for two hours on the address Jansen had given Blu, Crome hit pay dirt when their client took a drive at nine o'clock. Crome followed the man's big Audi from his Isle of Palms address into the city, crossing over the rickety old Cooper River Bridge. Locals weren't fazed by its gentle swaying and narrow lanes as they gunned across the landmark that should have been condemned a long time ago. Tourists could be spotted by their speed, or lack of it, as they tiptoed over the metal structure well below the thirty-five mile per hour speed limit.

Jansen got off at the Meeting Street exit and threaded his way into the city. Thanks to all the out of town traffic, Crome was able to keep him in sight and watch as he parallel parked at a meter on a side street.

Crome cursed, found a spot a block over, and double-timed it back to see their client walk into one of the nicer restaurants in the city. There was no way he could follow him in wearing his usual biker garb.

The best he could hope for was Jansen sitting at a table on the patio or at a window. He got lucky again when, after making a second pass in front of the brick building built before the Civil War, he spotted Jansen taking a seat across from a woman at an open window.

"Gotcha," Crome said. He moved to the other side of the street, pulled an automatic camera out of his pocket, used the zoom, and snapped ten shots. Darkness had been his friend and he stuck to the shadows.

The woman was, in Crome's opinion, spectacular—long, dark, curly hair; skin a natural shade of brown that was not exactly Middle Eastern or African or Latina, but a mixture of at least two of them; and the brightest smile he'd seen in a long time. He felt a longing for the woman and a wish for a piano to drop on Jansen flashed through his mind until he remembered the man was their paying client.

He used the other item Blu had issued him, a cell phone, and called his partner.

Blu answered the call. "You get something?"

"I've got our Mr. Jansen, economic advisor to the stars, having dinner with a hot babe as we speak." He told him the name of the restaurant.

"You get pictures?"

"Yep."

"Good," Blu said. "You see a ring on her finger?"

"To tell you the truth," Crome said, "I haven't made it down that far yet."

"Well, unglue your eyes from wherever they're stuck and look."

"That doesn't mean if she doesn't have one on she didn't take it off to meet Romeo, I mean Jansen."

"True, and she could be his sister for all we know."

Crome took another look at her dark skin and curly hair. "Not by birth. Or at least not by both parents."

"She Chinese or something?" Blu asked.

"Or something. Not Asian, I'm pretty sure of that."

"Keep it in your pants, Crome. We need this client to stay alive at least long enough to pay us the balance. I'm on my way."

"Roger that." Crome snapped the clamshell shut and stuck the phone in his pocket. Before his nap earlier, it had been two days since he'd slept. He slipped a small bottle of red pills out of a pocket, opened it, and swallowed one dry. With that, he'd be good for the remainder of his shift. Then he planned on crashing hard again.

Blu had been asleep when Crome called. The buzz of the phone on the dresser woke both him and Abby. With the problems they'd been having, sleep was better than fighting. At least he was getting rest.

He swung his legs off the side of the bed and sat up.

Abby grunted, rolled over, and fell back asleep. She was used to him coming and going at odd hours. Otherwise they wouldn't have lasted this long.

He dressed in black jeans and a black t-shirt, gave Hope a kiss on the forehead, and slipped on his shoes as he exited his house.

The mosquitoes buzzed around him, but they usually didn't bite.

He got in his truck, started the motor, looked in the rearview mirror as he selected reverse, and caught sight of a figure in the backseat. Quick as lightning he slipped his Beretta out of its holster. But the man in the backseat simply put something metal against Blu's head.

The man said, "Let's not do anything rash, okay?"

In the movie *Heavy Metal*, the taxi driver in the futuristic city had a foot controlled button that vaporized anyone in the backseat who threatened him. Blu wished he had the same gadget in his aging Cherokee at this moment.

He said, "Your call."

With the gun still to Blu's head, the man said, "Keep your gun. Now, get this heap moving."

Instead of holstering his gun, Blu set it on the passenger seat.

He backed out of his drive, and headed toward Seventeen which would take him into Charleston. And to Crome. In the rearview mirror, he noticed the man wore a mask. "Any place in particular?"

The man said, "You're heading there now."

"I am?"

"Yes. Your partner called and told you Mr. Jansen was in the restaurant having dinner with a woman."

Blu checked the rearview mirror again. "Is she your wife?"

The man sighed. "Just drive."

Crome lowered the tailgate on a pickup truck parked at a meter a few cars up from the restaurant and took a seat. The worst case was the owners of the truck came back before Jansen finished his dinner, got one look at Crome, and wouldn't say much. He'd hop off and they'd leave.

It wasn't as if he was hurting anything just sitting there.

In fact, with the little red pill taking effect, his mind focused on several things at once: the woman's naked ring finger, Jansen's demeanor, and the papers they appeared to be looking over. The ones with the staple in the upper left corner that resembled something he'd gotten so tired of in the Army—reports.

Crome tried Blu again on his cell but it rang out to voicemail. Either he was getting dressed, or talking to someone else or driving, or a combination thereof. He'd wanted this to be the mistress so they could get to the next phase of their investigation which was identifying the person or persons tailing Mr. Jansen. That would help them determine how to protect the weasel. Unfortunately, this was a business dinner and Crome and Blu would have to start over.

"You want to tell me why you're in the back seat of my truck pointing a gun at me?" It was a reasonable question, Blu thought.

The man took a deep breath and exhaled.

Blu caught a whiff of peppermint.

Finally, his passenger said, "I'm not pointing a gun at you anymore."

"But you still have it and you're still in the backseat of my truck."

"Is this your idea of trying to get on my good side so maybe I'll start liking you and we can bond and pretend that we could be best friends when all this is over?"

"When all of what is over?" Blu asked.

"You don't even know what is going on."

Blu said, "Why don't you tell me?"

The man coughed. "You think Jansen's screwing my wife? Is that the story he told you? That he's having an affair and the woman's husband is after him?"

"What do you think?"

No reply came.

Blu crossed over the Ashley River and entered the city. "First tell me where you want me to go?"

"You're meeting your partner, right? Don't change your plans on my account."

The man obviously didn't know Crome very well. One look at the situation and Crome would pull his three-fifty-seven and blow the masked man's head off.

Blu slowed for a red light. "We're almost there. Why don't you tell me what you think my client should have told me?"

The man said, "It isn't about a woman and jealous husband. There's a lot of money at stake. But it's at the expense of our environment. They want to bring cruise ships to town. I don't want that. They pollute the air, require deeper channels be cut into the rivers, and dump God knows what into the waters. I want Jansen to stop what he's doing. And I have powerful friends who will do whatever it takes to make it happen."

When the truck stopped, the man opened the back door, jumped out, and ran.

Blu turned his gaze to track him, but he was gone.

Chapter Twelve

October 2000

Crome watched as Blu's SUV idled up beside him.

Blu said, "Going my way?"

"You wish." Crome took a drag from a cigarette.

Pointing to the open spot in front of the pickup Crome was using as a bench, Blu asked, "You want me to park?"

"Yeah."

Blu pulled past the spot, reversed in, and inched forward, perfectly centering his truck in the space. He got out and joined Crome.

"Show-off."

Giving him a quick grin, Blu said, "Let me guess, it's a business dinner."

Crome eyed him. "Now how in the hell did you know that?"

"A masked man with a gun who rode with me into town in the backseat of my truck told me."

"No kidding?"

"No kidding," Blu said. "Something else, I think we're being watched right now."

Crome asked, "What the hell did you get us into this time?"

"Three days' worth of income. I don't care what Jansen's into. We're hired to protect him so that's what we're gonna do."

"No matter what?"

Blu watched their client talk to the woman. Crome was right, she was extraordinarily beautiful. "I didn't put any exceptions in the contract. You stay on him tonight and I'll pick it up tomorrow morning. See if this discussion turns romantic."

Crome said, "God, I hope not."

"Remember, Jansen's the one paying us. Keep your eyes on him, not her dress." Blu pulled out a hard pack of Camels, opened the lid, took one out, and lit it with the matches from the Pirate's Cove. Fanning the match out, he said, "I don't care what you do with her after this is over, but we've got to keep our heads in the game in this case. The man in my backseat said there was a lot of money at stake. Something about it being at the expense of the environment."

Crome pointed toward the window where their client could be seen paying for the check with a credit card. "You want to know something interesting about the woman?"

"This should be good."

"She doesn't eat like an American."

"What do you mean?" Blu asked.

"She uses both her knife and fork. Like a European."

Picking up subtle details was what kept them in this business. Both of them knew that something like that could be important, or it could be like chasing a rabbit down a hole. Crome had the feeling it was important or he wouldn't have mentioned it.

They both watched Jansen and the woman get up from the table. A minute later, he and the woman both exited the front door together. Outside, their conversation got what appeared to be heated. Then, the woman turned and walked away.

Jansen watched her for a moment and then headed in a different direction.

Crome said, "As much as I want to, you better follow the woman. My guess is she's heading to a hotel."

Blu knew Crome was right. Most likely, Jansen was heading home. The woman was now the important target. And Blu had a better chance getting close to her without setting off any alarms than a biker like Crome.

Whatever he found out about the woman, he'd let Crome know. With things on the rocks with Abby, all Blu needed was to be caught in a compromising situation with another female. Especially one as beautiful as this one.

He followed her, keeping half a block distance between them. Downtown Charleston in the tourist district was a lot of things, but dangerous wouldn't be a typical description. Still, any woman walking alone at night was always at risk.

Without her realizing it, Blu had taken up the role of protector. If anyone tried to make a move on her, it would be the last act of their life.

She walked two blocks and entered the hotel lobby of Charleston Place, an upscale establishment that also housed a shopping mall. It spanned the distance between King and Meeting Streets and had created quite a buzz when it was constructed fourteen years earlier.

After she cleared the door, Blu double-timed it to close the distance. The last thing he wanted to do was lose her in the lobby.

Inside, he caught a glimpse of her flowing, brown hair as she entered the restaurant.

Blu followed her in, watching as she avoided four men standing at one end of the bar and took a seat at the other.

The maitre d', a man dressed in black similar to Blu said, "Table for one?"

With a smile, Blu said, "I think I'll just sit at the bar."

The man extended his arm as both a welcome and to show him where it was. Blu thanked him and made his way over, slipping his wedding band off his hand and into his pocket. He took one of the stools that split the difference between the four men and the woman.

The men gave him what could be best described as sneers for what he believed they thought was intruding on their mark.

His pistol was underneath his untucked t-shirt but not really hidden from anyone trained to look for such things. These men were not trained in anything other than being self-important. As Blu situated himself in the seat, placing his phone, a pack of cigarettes, and a book of matches on the bar, the bartender, a man about Blu's age, late twenties, with slicked back hair, a white shirt, and black tie, stood a martini glass in front of the woman and asked him what he'd like.

"Tonic and lime."

The bartender said, "Gin?"

Blu declined and took a cigarette out of his pack. He picked up the matches and was about to light his smoke when the woman—the target—said, "I love that place."

She had a slight accent that Blu couldn't identify and she pointed to his matchbook.

Grinning, she said, "I spent the day at the beach and stopped in there for a late lunch."

His mind raced, not from a lack of understanding of what needed to be done, but from the reality of it all.

"I was there earlier today, myself," he said. "We must have just missed each other."

"The bird was, how do you say? Beautiful." She took a sip of her drink.

God, this woman was gorgeous. Any other time in his life, he would have considered this the best of luck. But now, with a marriage going south and a daughter taking collateral damage, he silently kicked himself for this good fortune.

"Yeah, the red and blue one. I can't believe the owner lets it fly around like that."

She said, "I know. It's one of the things I love about this city."

"Where are you from?"

"Amsterdam."

Now was the time to make the play and he regretted it immensely when he motioned to the seat next to her and said, "Do you mind?"

The reply was a very beautiful, full-lipped smile and nod that was more of an invitation of good things coming his way than he wanted or needed right now.

He took the seat, glancing at the men who shot multiple glare-darts back.

The woman held out her hand. "I'm Grietje." She pronounced it Griy-Tyeh.

Blu played it straight, giving her his real name as he put down his cigarette and shook her offered hand. Her skin was soft and warm and—

"Nice to meet you, Blu." Her eyes were all smiles. "Do you live here?"

"Across the river in West Ashley."

Lifting her glass, she said, "To the most beautiful city in America."

Blu couldn't argue with that. He clinked his glass with her Manhattan.

"So what brought you here?" he asked.

"Work. Always work."

Now for the money question. "What kind of work do you do?"

"International law."

An international lawyer meeting with an economic advisor. Made sense.

"Is your work over for the week?"

She frowned. "Hardly. So what do you do?"

He handed her a card. "Private security."

The bright smile returned. "Really? Like bodyguards and guns?"

"Yes."

Leaning in closer now, she said, "Do you like guarding bodies?"

He returned her smile. "It pays the bills."

"Now, that's not what I asked."

He offered a cigarette, which she took, and lit it for her.

"Okay," he said, "you're right. Some people I like more than others, but I treat them all the same. Business is business and money is all the same color."

"Are you good at your job?" she asked.

There was only one real answer to that question. Actually, there were two answers. He gave them. "I'm still alive and I haven't lost a client under my protection yet."

She took a drag from her cigarette, exhaled, and lifted her glass signaling for the bartender to give her a second drink.

Blu decided to go all in. "I'm on a job right now."

Her eyes cut sideways to him. "But I didn't pay you to guard my body."

"No. Mr. Jansen paid me to guard his."

Without hesitation, she said, "I thought so. You think I am here to hurt him?"

Blu inhaled a lungful of smoke and blew it away from her, toward the four men still glaring at him. "You tell me."

"He said there were probably men watching him and that someone might approach me." She put her hand on Blu's arm. "I appreciate that you did not lie to me."

He smiled again. "You didn't answer my question."

"Like you, I work for others. They pay me so I represent them to the best of my ability, whether I like them or not."

"You don't like your employer?"

Lifting her hand off his arm, she took the drink from the bartender, gave her glass a slight raise, and then took a drink. "I'm not here to hurt Mr. Jansen. But my employer has an agenda and there are some conflicts."

"The pen is mightier than the sword."

"In this case," she said, "much mightier."

Blu fought in Desert Storm which he learned was paid for by the Saudis in an oil grab. Swords killed people but the really powerful men crushed nations and corporations with backroom deals. It was all above his pay grade.

She took a last drag off her cigarette, exhaled, and stubbed the smoke out in an ashtray. "So, Blu Carraway of Blu Carraway Investigations, would you care to guard my body for the remainder of the evening? I could use a break from my work and a nice tour of your city would be quite lovely."

"I'm expensive."

"So am I," she said. "That is why I can afford whatever you wish to charge."

His mind filled with flashes of Abby and Hope. At this moment, he understood something that had been haunting him— even if he lost Abby, and it looked that way, he'd always have Hope.

Blu reached for his money fold to pay for their drinks.

Grietje put her hand on his arm again. "This is business."

It was a true statement.

She handed the bartender a charge card. "My company pays."

"For me as well?" he asked.

She gave him a sideways, cocked head look. "I think I'll take care of you personally."

The bartender returned with the card and bill for her to sign.

Blu's phone buzzed in his pocket. He looked at the display, saw the number for the phone Crome used, and let it go to voicemail. Then he sent Crome a quick text: *On target.* If he didn't respond, Crome might get concerned, leave Jansen, and come looking.

He stood, helped her move her stool back so she could step away from the bar, and smiled at the four men still standing at the other end with nothing but their drinks in their hands.

One of them said, "Have a nice evening."

It didn't really sound genuine to Blu, but he let it slide.

After Blu held the door open for her to leave, they stood on the cracked concrete. In Charleston, all of the sidewalks had fissures.

Grietje said, "I am all yours, as they say, Mr. Bodyguard."

With a wave of his hand, he motioned for her to join him and they walked up the sidewalk toward the harbor. She didn't say anything for quite a while. Blu could sense someone following, but he couldn't spot them.

He'd lived in the city for a few years and his job had taken him down some dark alleys. His clients sometimes came from the cracks in the foundation of decent society. Those cracks were under a city going on four centuries old—dark places populated by palmetto bugs and roof rats and characters on the fringes.

Grietje told him her home now was Hamburg, Germany. While in the Army, Blu had spent time in Hamburg, and a few nights best forgotten on the famous Reeperbahn, Hamburg's red-light district. She would know about cockroaches and vermin. And she might also know how to work in their midst.

Taking a short cut to the Battery, Blu cut down Simmons Alley, found himself walking alone, and heard Grietje say something. When he turned to look at her, he saw she spoke into a cell phone.

She lowered the phone. "I'm sorry, Mr. Blu Carraway, Private Investigator. It's time for us to part ways."

He caught movement to his left.

The Rangers had taught him quite a bit about self preservation. Their regimental motto was Sua Sponte. The Latin saying meant "of their own accord." It recognized that a Ranger volunteered three times: for the U.S. Army, for Airborne School, and for service in the 75th Ranger Regiment. And it also referred to the Ranger's self-reliance.

Blu had been a model Ranger.

Within two seconds, he held his Beretta in one hand and lifted Grietja over his shoulder like a sack of potatoes with the other.

Bent over at the waist, she covered his back as he made his way to the exit with the hope that her team would not shoot if there was a risk of hitting her.

She squirmed and bucked and punched at his back and kidneys. The blows were hard, but worth the bruising. Bullets were less forgiving.

He exited the alley at the other end, turned the corner, and made his way up Chalmers Street.

A quarter block up, he dumped her into the bed of a parked pickup with a loud thump and ran. Footsteps of several figures following sounded on the stone sidewalk. He double-timed it to East Bay Street and found a decent-sized crowd of tourists.

Slipping his gun down the back waistband of his jeans, Blu did his best to use the crowd for cover. Grietje's attempted set-up told him Crome and Jansen might also be in danger. Ducking into the patio of one of the more popular watering holes set at an intersection, he grabbed a two-top table in a back corner with a perfect view of the sidewalk. Thirty seconds later, while a waitress took his order of a sweet iced tea with a frown, he noticed two men walking with purpose on the sidewalk. Although dressed like tourists in ironed polo shirts and khaki shorts, they were too fit and determined to really be.

After the waitress left to get his drink and the men had passed, Blu took out his phone and called Crome.

"Yo."

"Watch your six," Blu said. "Your girlfriend was a setup."

Crome said, "No kidding."

"They've been a step ahead of us the entire time. The man riding into town with me should have been a tip-off. Where are you?"

Crome told him he had just watched Jansen pull into his driveway.

"I think our man is in for it."

Chapter Thirteen

Monday night, October 2000

The previous night, Blu found out that Jansen's house was elevated on stilts because it stood across the street from the beach front homes, making it what the locals called "second row." It was a way of explaining hierarchical status without coming out and saying the man was wealthy, but not "front row" mega-rich. Many of the commoners had already moved off the island, no longer able to afford the property tax.

While the location might be considered desirable from a real estate perspective, it wasn't easy to secure. With a road in front and neighbors on the three remaining sides, one man could not easily cover it.

Crome suggested they get some help.

Blu was hesitant, if only because Crome sometimes associated with characters on the outskirts of decent society. It wasn't who they were that bothered Blu, or being around them. The job took them all over the place and their paths intersected with all kinds of people. It was the liability of having a few more men like Crome on this job. The wrong men could get them in over their heads real fast.

As if reading his mind, Crome said, "You pick them."

Irritating Crome wasn't Blu's intention when he took him up on the suggestion and hired two off-duty police officers to moonlight with them. It was just a bonus. Sort of like retribution for fornicating with Daron on the couch in the office and almost jeopardizing the job before they got the contract.

To his credit, Crome kept his tongue in check. One of the officers was Roger Powers, Blu's good friend. He didn't just pick anyone to work with them. The extra help was quality, not quantity.

Powers, in uniform, sat on the couch while Blu explained the job. His partner, a rookie named Les Griffith, sat beside him. Both were in their late twenties like Blu and Crome, both eager to make their mark, and both familiar with the city. Griffith was a dark-skinned African American, about five ten, and stocky. Powers was a trim but not thin six-foot white guy.

They split up into two teams, Blu and Powers and Crome and Griffith. And then by shifts. Crome and Griffith were night owls. Blu and Powers had families so they preferred the day shift.

It happened when Crome and Griffith were staking out the elevated house. Crome was on one side and Griffith had the opposite corner. A silver Infiniti pulled into Jansen's drive. Crome used one of his sources to run the plate, not wanting Griffith to get in trouble because he'd done it while on a private gig.

Two men exited the car, walked up the stairs, and approached the door.

While they waited for Jansen to answer their knock, the information on the plate came back that it belonged on a Volkswagen in the system as reported stolen. That was all Crome needed. He radioed Griffith. They jumped out of their cars and approached the house from their respective sides.

Jansen answered the door as Crome rounded the porch. He yelled, "Get down."

The men at the door turned and drew down on Crome.

Griffith approached from the opposite side and they didn't see him. He said, "Police! Hands up!"

Instead of following the command, the men crouched low and pushed their way into the house.

Crome realized the mistake he and Griffith had made. They shouldn't have let the men get to the house. It hadn't felt right to him but he'd played it too safe and it had cost him, and maybe Jansen's life.

The two men inside could defend the house. Crome decided to take the fight up a notch. He signaled for Griffith to cover the back of the house and ducked behind the Infiniti, pulling his Ka-Bar knife.

The fuel tank was made from plastic and he punctured holes in it, letting the gasoline drain onto the driveway.

Then he lit the puddle off and ran the other way.

The car blew up beautifully. An explosion replaced the darkness with illumination. In the afterglow, Crome wondered if the neighborhood had ever experienced anything like that before.

Probably not, and now the inhabitants' safe and secure upper-middle-class lives would never be the same.

Welcome to the new world.

Gunfire erupted out of the front windows.

It would only be a matter of time before the police showed up. And the fire department. And then the reporters. This would be a hot story in the sleepy lowcountry.

Crome let the men inside expend their ammo.

The police could handle it from here. All he and Griffith had to do was make sure the men didn't escape out some back door or side window.

The car fire in the driveway put off quite a bit of light which helped them cover the house.

His cell phone buzzed. It was Griffith. Crome answered and the guy said, "My friends are on their way. I don't want to be here when they show up."

Crome said, "The keys are in the Honda. Circle toward the front of the house and I'll take your place. Get in the car but wait until you see the lights coming. We need to cover the house so the two idiots inside don't sneak out."

"Roger that."

*   *   *

Blu slid a Camel out of the pack and lit up with the Pirate's Cove matches. What he had here was a Class A screw up: an exploded car in the driveway of a home in the wealthy part of town, multiple gunshots fired, a hostage situation, and his partner sitting on the hood of their other incognito Honda grinning like a first grader.

After exhaling a lungful of mild Turkish blend, Blu asked what was an obvious question to himself, if not others. "Did you have to blow up their car?"

His business partner didn't bother to hide his chuckle.

"What's so funny?" Blu asked.

"You," Crome said. "Our client is inside with those two idiots who couldn't hit water if they fell out of a boat and all you're worried about is some torched Infiniti."

Blu looked toward the house. The fire department was busy hosing off the rubble that was a nice car before Crome blew it up. Five police cars parked haphazard in front, their blue lights bouncing off the siding of the surrounding homes. Two officers stood behind the open doors of their cruiser, one of them with a bullhorn.

Using the bullhorn, the officer said, "Release Mr. Jansen now before anyone gets hurt."

The response from the house was silence.

The officer tried again. "You want to consider dealing with us before the suits get here. Once that happens, we can't help you anymore."

Blu's cell phone vibrated in his pocket. He checked the number, didn't recognize it, and answered.

Grietje said, "Guess who I have?"

This really wasn't good at all.

"What do you want?" Blu asked.

"Cooperation. Keep the police busy. I'll call you back." She ended the call.

With a nod, Blu signaled Crome to follow him as he stepped

farther away from the organized chaos that was the scene of the crime.

Once out of earshot of any of the officers, Blu said, "The woman has Jansen."

His partner's smile vanished as Blu watched him think about what he'd just heard.

After a few beats, Crome said, "These people are real good. They must have gone out the back door with our boy right at the start. Those shots were just decoys."

"You mean you didn't return fire?"

"Hell no," Crome said. "I didn't want to risk hitting Jansen."

At least he'd kept his head about him.

Blu stubbed out his cigarette. "How'd they get off the island if you blew up their car?"

Crome lit a Winston, took a drag, held the cigarette between two fingers on his right hand, and used it to point it at Blu. "They had a backup plan which kicked in as soon as it exploded."

"These guys are professionals," Blu said.

"They got us on this one, partner."

Chapter Fourteen

The next morning, Tuesday, October 2000

Blu and Crome left the scene when the police and fire department finished restoring law and order. It helped that Crome had developed amnesia when it came to how the car blew up, hinting that it must have been the guys who'd taken Jansen. While sabotage was obvious and spontaneous combustion unlikely, there were no other witnesses to offer alternative theories.

The closest place to regroup and wait for Grietje's call was the Pirate's Cove bar which opened at ten. They walked in and the one-eyed bartender, Reggie Sails, greeted them from behind the bar.

The song playing on the juke was Clapton's "Wonderful Tonight." If only it had been.

"You fellas look like you need drinks," he said. "I heard a car blew up. And now you're here. Must be a coincidence."

"Must be," Crome said. "Gimme a draft and a double shot of Crown."

"Sweet tea," Blu said.

The old man took care of Crome first and then placed a pint glass of tea with two lemon wedges stuck on the rim in front of Blu.

The grungy bar was not very busy at the moment. Four shirtless college-aged guys shot pool at the worn table in the corner. Two co-eds, both of them potential cheerleader material with bikini tops and cut-off jean shorts, watched the pool players.

Crome popped a red and washed it down with his shot.

The old man said, "Those things'll catch up with you one day."

With a grin, Crome said, "Only if I stop."

Blu pulled his cell phone out and sat it on the bar in front of him.

"So will those things," the old man said, holding a plastic tipped cigar and pointing at the phone. "Don't want nothin' to do with 'em."

"I don't blame you," Crome said.

The juke switched to "Surfin' Safari" by the Beach Boys.

To Crome, Blu said, "You got phone duty. I'm goin' for a swim."

"What the—" Crome started to say.

Blu took a swig from his tea, got off the stool, and left the bar. Next door was a souvenir shop that looked like it was new. And open. He walked in and was immediately hit by the smell of cheap rubber and plastic. At a rack against the wall, Blu found a pair of swim shorts his size. On his way to the register, he picked up a bright-colored beach towel that had been marked down along with a discounted pair of flip-flops.

The cashier, a plump teenaged girl, smacked her lips on gum while she rang up his order.

Outside, a block down from the store, was a public restroom and changing area.

Blu changed, put his clothes in the plastic bag that still had the towel, and walked the bridge over the dunes to the surf. He dropped the bag onto the sand, kicked his flops off, and jogged into the waves.

The water felt warm and soothed the aches of the bad night.

In college, Blu had competed with the swim team and had a powerful stroke. He charged out to sea until his smoker's lungs screamed. And then he pushed thirty more seconds before turning around and heading back.

As he approached the shore and his toes touched sand, he stood and wiped water from his face and short-cropped hair.

Crome stood by his towel and smoked a cigarette. "Your

girlfriend called."

Blu picked up his stuff and headed for the shower and changing room. "What'd she say?"

"I told her you were takin' a swim. She asked if you were single."

"Quit jerkin' around, Crome. What's the plan?"

"Hey, partner," Crome said, "I wasn't the one who decided to take a mini vacation in the middle of this situation that could best be described as FUBAR."

Blu stood under the outdoor shower and let the cold water wash the salt and sand from his skin. When he finished, he stepped inside the public restrooms, dried off with the towel, changed back into his clothes, and was ready to go.

His partner used reds to keep his edge. Blu preferred a more holistic approach. The ocean would always be the best place to clear one's head, in his opinion. And when he couldn't swim, he went to the gym.

Outside the public restrooms, Blu asked again, "So what's the plan?"

"She thinks she has the upper hand. I'm inclined to agree with her."

"Why? Because she has Jansen?"

Crome turned his head from side to side as if regarding Blu as the village idiot. Perhaps he was.

Blu opened the chamber of his nine millimeter and blew in it in case any sand had gotten inside.

"She wants you to call her back. Wouldn't talk to me. I offered to let her talk to that big parrot Reggie's got in the bar and she hung up."

"I guess I gotta give her a call."

"Is what I been tryin' to tell ya." Crome handed him the phone.

"Using a heck of a lot of words, Crome." He snatched the phone. "Not everyone likes to hear the sound of your voice as much as you do."

"Why the hell not?"

Blu hit redial and Grietje answered with, "I considered shooting Jansen."

"What stopped you?"

"Curiosity," she replied.

"Because I didn't answer your call?"

"Yes."

Well, la-di-freakin-da.

"What do you want?" he asked.

"Clean oceans. World peace."

"You sure have a funny way of showing the second one."

She laughed. It was a nice laugh, and remembering her beauty was distracting. She had, after all, set him up to be shot and had kidnapped his client.

"You didn't ask the right question, Mr. Blu Carraway, Private Investigator."

"What's the right question?"

"When you think of it," she said, "call me back."

The call ended.

Crome had been watching Blu. He said, "Well?"

Blu stood there with the phone in his hand and his mind absolutely vacant of what to say.

"Blu?"

He snapped out of it, and said, "I have to think of the right question to ask and then call her back."

"You want to say that again?"

"You heard me." Blu just couldn't believe it.

Crome said, "You asked her what she wanted and she said that wasn't the right question."

"Yep."

"Then it's not what she wants that's the question."

Most people never looked past Crome's biker wardrobe to get to know the man. If they had, they would understand that his mind was always running. Some might say it was the reds, and there was truth in that. But the man was dangerously intelligent.

Blu said, "I know it's not what she wants."

"No," Crome said. "It's not what she wants. Meaning it's most likely what her handler wants. She wants you to think of her as a go-between, as crazy as that sounds. I think she likes you, partner."

"Why do I always get the whack jobs?" A bitter feeling escaped when he said it. He immediately thought of Abby and felt ashamed at thinking of the mother of his daughter that way.

"Because," Crome said as he put a hand on Blu's shoulder, "you got that Latin swagger that drives 'em wild."

"Thanks a lot."

"Don't mention it."

Blu hit redial.

"Yes?" Grietje answered.

"What do they want?"

"Smart man," she said. "I knew you'd figure it out. They want Mr. Jansen to agree to their terms. Once he does, he will be released."

"You expect me to believe that?"

"Yes," she said. "I would not lie to you."

"How about you and I finish our walk around the city?" he asked.

"I'd love to," she said. "Except that I'm not convinced you wouldn't lie to me."

"And your friends would be around to make sure I was a gentleman."

He heard her laugh again.

"There you go again assuming you know what I want."

The call ended.

Crome said, "Well hell's bells, what's next?"

Chapter Fifteen

October 2000

Blu had an idea what was next. He just couldn't believe he was thinking it.

"Jansen's also playing a game."

Crome coughed out smoke from his cigarette. "Why?"

"Think about it," Blu said. "He goes in his house. You guys are practically on top of him. And he's kidnapped? Grietje's men are not that good—we should know. It's the only explanation."

"So he pays us to dupe us?"

"No." Blu had to think about his answer. It still didn't make complete sense, but his hunch felt right. "Something's missing. We don't know the reason yet."

Crome flicked ashes off his smoke. "So what are we supposed to do now? Forget about our client and hope you're right?"

With a smile, Blu said, "We're going to play along. I'll call Grietje tomorrow."

"Before you forget," Crome said, "you're still married."

Blu heard his partner, and at the same time didn't hear him.

Hope looked up at her father with the eyes of an angel. They were his eyes, but were filled with her spirit. And they were perfect.

Blu lifted her up and kissed her on the forehead. "How's my

girl?"

"Good, now." She rubbed her nose on his.

Abby said, "We haven't seen you for two days, Blu."

It always came back to this—his job. The source of their income while she finished her nursing classes. He had a feeling after she graduated, sooner or later, she'd leave and take Hope with her.

"I'm sorry," he said. "Someone kidnapped our client."

"How'd they do that, Daddy?"

He said, "They were sneakier than me and Uncle Crome. But we'll get him back. We always do."

Hope chanted, "We always do! We always do! We always do!"

Abby took her from Blu. "Come on, Sweetie. It's bedtime."

"No!" Tears ran down her face.

One moment she's happy. The next, she's miserable. Such was the life of a three-year-old.

Blu watched his wife take their crying daughter to bed and got a glass and filled it from the kitchen faucet. Abby liked the bottled stuff. Blu was just a tap water kind of guy. And that wasn't going to be good enough for her in the long run. He couldn't remember the last time they had a quiet moment together, much less made love.

His phone buzzed.

He looked at the display, saw Grietje's number, and thought tonight wouldn't be any better for his marriage.

Grietje stared at him from her seat at the bar, giving him her full-lipped smile, as if she'd never tried to have him killed.

"Miss You" by the Rolling Stones played in the background.

Blu pulled two cigarettes, lit them with the Pirate's Cove matches, and gave one to her.

She took the offered smoke between two long slender fingers, held it to her mouth, and inhaled a lungful. Blowing out a steady stream to the ceiling, she smiled. "I'm surprised you would want to see me again."

"To tell you the truth," he said, "I'm not sure I'm thinking clearly."

Fingering the stem of her wine glass, she hesitated before speaking. "My men wouldn't have killed you."

Using the same hand that held his cigarette, Blu picked up the tumbler of club soda, raised it to her, and took a drink, not believing a word of what she just said.

"You don't trust me, do you?" she asked.

"Not at all, but it's a nice thought."

"What is?" she asked, leaning in. "Thinking that I wouldn't have you killed, or wanting to accept what I say to you as truth?"

The halo of the dim lighting around her curls made him want to touch them. He said, "You didn't enjoy it very much when I carried you down the street."

She sat back and hooked an elbow behind the backrest of her barstool, retreating but still open to him. "You find that funny, don't you?"

"Not at the time." But thinking about it now: her weight over his shoulder, the closeness of her, and the smell of her perfume on his clothes afterward.

"Probably not," she said. "But now, here facing me. You're thinking about it and liking what you did. How you handled me."

"Lady," he said.

"You know my name." She moved toward him again, getting in close. "It's Grietje."

He didn't blink. "I know what you said your name is."

Nose to nose, like he'd been with Hope, but nothing like he was with his daughter, Grietje said, "I'm just the person in the middle. I'm not bad. I'm just doing my job."

With noses still touching, he said, "You've been doing this for too long."

With a slight head tilt, but still making skin contact, she said, "What do you mean?"

"You're so good at lying that you can lie to yourself."

She put a hand on his shoulder and guided him in for a kiss.

He didn't resist. Hell, he wanted this. And a distant part of him, deep inside, said he'd also been doing this for too long because he didn't care anymore.

Crome sat alone and nursed a pint and his pack of Winstons while he watched his partner across the room. The woman really was beautiful. She'd flipped some switch in him when he first saw her with Jansen. And now she was using her beauty to hoodwink his partner. The worst part was it worked.

When the woman pulled Blu in close, Crome said *sotto voce*, "Oh, no."

There were a lot of things Crome could do. Try to call his partner on his cell phone, see if the poor sap would actually answer the call with that woman's hands all over him. He could walk up to them, slap his partner on the back, and remind him he was still married. Yell from where he sat. Pull out his Beretta and fire a warning shot.

He did none of those things.

Blu could be crazy, unpredictable, and often totally wrong. But the ladies loved him.

Blu didn't know how far this was going to go. Grietje seemed to want to take it over the edge. He wanted to find his client.

There didn't appear to be any middle ground.

They left the bar and made it to her hotel room. Blu realized he was way past the line of sense and sensibility.

Except for one detail: Crome.

Blu was putting quite a bit of confidence in his partner exercising good judgment and stepping in to save him from himself. It might not have been the best of plans. The phone in his pocket buzzed. He checked the display and found the number he and Crome had agreed upon for "all clear."

The room was actually a suite with a large sitting area next to the bed. She made herself a drink from an already opened bottle of bourbon, kicked off her shoes, and sat on a couch.

"Why am I really here?" he asked.

She patted the cushion next to her. "Take a seat."

Blu sat next to, but not beside her. "I want to talk to my client."

"Impossible." She sipped her drink.

"Call your handler and hand me the phone."

"He already knows you're here. Ron hasn't agreed to the terms, yet."

"So, again, why am I here?"

"Because," she said, "I don't want you out there looking for him."

"You think you've got me locked up?"

"My team is close by. You're not going anywhere."

He said, "I think you might have overestimated yourself."

She paused from taking another drink. "What does that mean?"

"It means that I've got a man outside your door. I've got a van waiting down at the curb. And I've got a place a lot less comfortable than this where you'll be while I look for Jansen."

"You think you can take me?" she asked.

"It's what I'm good at," he said. "Making people disappear."

"And I thought we were getting along so well in the bar downstairs."

"We were," he said. "But you have my client and I want him back."

"What if I scream?"

Blu rapped on the wall. "This is old construction with solid beams and horsehair insulation. Scream all you want."

"My men will stop you."

With a smile, Blu said, "Your men are already out of the picture."

The turn in her expression was slight. The confidence of someone usually in control now wavering. Next would be anger and then fear. It didn't matter. Only getting his client back mattered.

Grietje tried to play it cool. She took another drink, set the glass on the coffee table in front of the couch, and ran her fingers through her hair.

If Blu hadn't had Abby and Hope to think about, he knew he'd have succumbed to Grietje's beauty. And if he didn't have Crome at his flank, he'd already be dead.

It was time to go back to church like his mother had taught him and thank God for keeping him alive these twenty-seven years.

He picked up her purse and took out a nice Ruger thirty-two which he stuck down the front of his jeans.

"You can have my lipstick too, if you want."

With a smile, he took a cell phone out of her purse and handed it to her. "Go ahead and make the call."

Chapter Sixteen

October 2000

Crome stood beside the panel van he'd rented for the evening. Inside were four men hog-tied and in various states of consciousness.

Propped up on the windshield wiper were four cell phones. One of them buzzed and he answered with, "Mick's cleaning service. We take the trash out."

"Who is this?" said a woman's voice. Hopefully, the woman Blu had gone upstairs with and wasn't having sex with at the moment.

He said, "Who's this?"

No answer.

"Listen, Grietje," he said. "I've got your men. I've got their phones. And I've got their guns. Tell Blu where Jansen is and I'll let them go. Play some game and I'm going to chop them into pieces and use them for crab bait."

The call ended.

He took a nice long drag from a Winston and chuckled.

Blu asked, "Who did you think you were playing with, here?"

When Grietje had ended the call, she sunk further into the couch. Whatever hope was left in her operation had vanished.

"You don't understand," she said. "He'll kill me."

"Me and my partner. We're who you have to worry about."

She looked at him. "You'd kill a woman?"

The truth was that neither he nor Crome would kill someone in her position. Not when they already had the upper hand.

He said, "I'll do whatever it takes to win this game."

Springing to her feet, Grietje tried to run for the door.

Blu grabbed her blouse and tugged hard. She sailed backwards and ended up back on the couch. "Don't try me. I need you alive right now. But that doesn't mean I won't hurt you." He ripped one of the sheer curtains down. "Stand up."

She stood and looked at him, trying for seduction again with big, bedroom eyes.

He turned her around.

She tried to slap him.

He gave her a thumb lock, putting pressure on the thumb joint and twisting her elbow back.

She yipped but he knew she couldn't move. He had her in complete control.

Then he shoved her back down onto the couch.

"I'm going to use your phone and call your handler. I want you to get him over here."

She spat at him. "I'm not doing anything for a man who likes to hurt women."

"You're lucky that's all you got." He bent down so he was eye to eye. "I don't like hurting women. But I've got lady-friends who would love to take turns turning that beautiful face of yours into something less attractive. And they work cheap."

It wasn't exactly a hollow threat. In his line of work, he met all kinds.

After a beat, she looked away, defeated if he had to guess.

"It's the second number in my call log," she said.

Blu hit the green button, got the list of previous calls and selected the number.

The phone was answered on the second ring by a voice who sounded a lot like the man that rode into town with him the previous night. "Did you take care of them?"

Instead of putting the phone to Grietje's cheek, Blu said, "She sure did."

"Who's this?"

"The man who gave you a lift into town the other night. I want to speak to Ron Jansen."

There was no reply.

"I've got Grietje and her operatives. They're still alive, but may not be much longer depending on how this conversation goes."

With more than a hint of panic, the man said, "Don't hurt her."

"She's okay so far."

Grietje screamed, "He hit me!"

The man said, "You hit her?"

"No," Blu said. "But I can. Do we understand each other?"

"Yes."

"Good. Meet me in Battery Park in one hour. With Jansen." Blu ended the call.

Grietje started to say something else.

Blu drew the Ruger and showed it to her.

She stopped.

At thirty-five minutes, Crome walked up the steps and knocked on the door to the hotel room.

Blu opened the door, waved him in, and said, "She's all yours."

"Looks like she's in one piece," Crome said, but thinking, she's even more spectacular up close.

Looking at Grietje, Blu said, "She knows she'll stay that way as long as she doesn't try anything stupid."

Crome said, "See you in a few."

Blu saluted and left.

Staring at the woman as she looked out a window, Crome said, "Why go through all this?"

There was no response. She didn't even bother to look at him.

Crome lit a Winston, took a drag, and then put it to her lips.

She inhaled and tilted her head back as if needing the nicotine jolt. Exhaling, "How are my men?"

"That depends."

Two were beat up pretty badly. The other two surrendered without too much of a fight.

"On what?" she asked.

He offered her another drag and she took it.

"On how long this takes before you can get them proper medical treatment."

"Cruel." She pronounced it with two syllables.

"And setting up my partner wasn't?"

She didn't reply, looking toward the window again.

"That's what I thought," he said. "Selective judgment."

"You don't understand. There is a lot at stake. This is big enough that people will do anything."

She went silent after that and Crome didn't feel the need to understand.

At the exact time Blu was to meet the man and Jansen, Crome untied Grietje and handed her purse back sans Ruger and phone.

She slung the bag over her shoulder and clenched her fists as if ready to come at him. Instead, she turned and left.

Jansen stood on the walkway overlooking the harbor when Blu walked up. The medium build man with his glasses and thinning hair had a weak smile that made him look vulnerable.

Blu asked, "Where's your captor?"

"He told me to tell you he can take you out anytime he wants to."

"What's all this about?"

Jansen sighed. "Cruise ships. I want them anchoring off our harbor but they don't."

"I thought you were an economic advisor, whatever that means."

"Tourism is big money. Cruise ships will bring it in by the

boatloads."

Blu asked, "So can we leave or what?"

"He said when he hears from the woman, he'll let us go."

A woman's voice said, "I'm right here, Mr. Jansen."

It was Grietje.

Blu turned to see her aim a gun at Jansen just as gunshots erupted and she fell forward, dropping the pistol in her hand. He caught her as she fell.

Jansen took off running.

More gunshots went off.

Crome approached, gun drawn, yelled, "Get down!" and shoved Blu and the woman to the ground.

People around them screamed.

Blu and Crome stood on the elevated part of the stone walkway overlooking the harbor. Battery Park, and its line of million-dollar homes, was directly behind them. Officer Powers, Blu's friend, stood nearby.

If Blu had to categorize the day, he'd say it started out well but ended up not so great. Crome shot Grietje because she was about to shoot Jansen. Whoever fired at them could not be found. Her handler was in the wind.

Turned out Grietje was part of an eco-terrorist organization called Marine Life Marines. While Blu appreciated the concept of protecting the oceans, he didn't see where this plot of theirs did anything besides get Grietje killed.

Ron Jansen escaped without harm. He was giving his statement to the police. Blu had a chance to talk with him before they'd arrived. The truth was there was no married woman. Jansen just wanted someone watching his back. He promised to pay Blu for seven twenty-four-hour days as a thank you for, what he called, "A job well done."

Blu was going to take the money, even if he didn't feel he'd really earned it.

Crome looked over at him, unfazed that he had just killed a woman. "Whatcha thinkin'?"

"If Jansen had told me the truth, Grietje would still be alive because it never would have gotten this far."

Exhaling a cloud of smoke and flicking his cigarette butt into the water, Crome said, "You want black and white. Life ain't ever black and white. It's all gray. A million shades of it. It's why we make a living. Besides, you really think we could handle some desk job?"

Crome took out another cigarette and lit up. "No, this is who we are, Blu. This is who we are."

Chapter Seventeen

Present time, McDonald's in Mount Pleasant, Tuesday evening

Blu stood outside the McDonald's, thinking hard about what he was going to say to his business partner. Crome was normally the smartest guy in the room, but recently he'd been acting like a complete jackass.

In any other situation, this would be grounds for dissolution of the partnership. But this wasn't any situation. Crome was all screwed up inside. He cared for Maureen and he wasn't used to caring for anything but his motorcycle. Blu had come to realize this was new to him.

Some whack job had taken her and only God knew how the man had been treating the poor woman.

So, with all that, Crome deserved the benefit of the doubt. He deserved help.

Blu stepped inside the McDonald's.

Crome watched as Blu took the bench seat across from him, neither of them saying anything for quite a long time.

After staring at his partner, Crome picked up his sandwich and continued to eat.

"How do you want to play it?" Blu asked.

It was typical of his partner to do exactly the opposite of what was expected. Like now. Crome knew his partner was livid. He'd spent a lot of time and effort tracking him. He said, "All the way."

Leaning forward, fingers laced, hands out in front of him, Blu said, "That's a given. You got me and Harmony and Tess and Patricia and Pelton and his wife. And you got this big chip on your shoulder."

Crome finished his sandwich. "Good. What have you got?"

Blu said, "I'd say we've arrived at the same place. Only I had to spend extra time tracking some tool who thought he didn't need any help."

Crome drank from his Coke, the liquid cavitating in the straw as the last of the drink got sucked down, the noise echoing in the restaurant. Setting the cup on the table, he said, "That's the difference between you and me, partner. I'dda known what you were doing and tried to work on what you weren't."

"Because you'd've known I wouldn't have done anything rash."

"You mean to tell me," Crome said, "that when those men took Hope that one time, you and the kid played by the rules?"

Blu didn't respond.

"It ain't as if I stashed Phineous someplace you couldn't find. That would have been stupid. Jesus, Blu. You always think the worst."

"No," Blu said. "I want to help my friend."

There wasn't anything Crome could say that would make Blu understand. Hell, he didn't really understand it himself.

"What do you suggest we do?" Blu asked.

Crome took out a piece of paper and set it on the table. "I got the people who stayed on the floor of the hotel where Maureen was held. All of the rooms have changed occupants at least once since I got the picture so I'm assuming she isn't there anymore."

Blu pulled out his own piece of paper and laid it over Crome's sheet.

"What's that?" Crome asked.

"The list of credit cards used to pay for the rooms."

Rule number one, follow the money.

Blu had been busy.

*   *   *

Blu's irritation with his partner went back a long time. He loved the man like a brother, but damn if Crome didn't always have to do things his own way. And he still hadn't forgiven Crome for talking him out of taking a six-figure security job—with benefits—because Crome couldn't be faithful to more than just his motorcycle. Sliding out of the booth, Blu said, "The ladies are working on getting more intel."

"Good," Crome said. "I got something else I need to follow up on."

"Really?" Blu asked. "You think I'm going to let you ride off and do your thing after I just found you?"

"Well," Crome said with an actual chuckle, "you showed yourself you can find me. I'm sure you can do it again if you really work at it." He stood.

This wasn't happening. Not this way. Blu wasn't going to let it. He got up in his partner's face, making him turn his back to the big plate glass window overlooking the parking lot. "You think that's how this is going to play out?"

Blu needed thirty seconds. That was five and counting.

"Get outta my way, partner," Crome said.

Ten seconds.

Blu grabbed his partner's vest. "No chance."

Fifteen seconds.

Crome pushed Blu backwards.

Eighteen seconds.

Blu's butt hit the table behind him, stopping Crome from pushing any further.

Twenty seconds.

He pushed back but Crome held firm.

Twenty-three seconds.

With both hands and what felt like all his strength, Crome lifted Blu off the ground.

Twenty-five seconds.

It went against all of Blu's training not to be beating his partner senseless right now.

Twenty-seven seconds.

Crome used his momentum and tossed Blu over a table and chairs.

Thirty seconds.

Blu landed hard but rebounded in time to see the door swing shut as Crome hiked a leg over his bike's saddle, fire off the motor, and roar away.

The thirty seconds was so Harmony's friend had time to plant a LoJack on Crome's bike. The guy who planted it did surveillance for the Charleston office of the DEA. Crome would not find the device with a ten second once-over.

As Crome wound out his Harley, a bad feeling came over him. Not about throwing his partner out of the way. It was that it had all been too easy. Blu was up to something.

Any other time, a real fight between him and his partner would have ended with two tickets to the emergency room.

He checked his mirrors. There were a lot of cars behind him. Memorizing their makes and models as best he could see, he'd check again in five minutes to see if any of the same were still behind him.

With Blu on the hotel gig, he could focus on the other aspect of this that bothered him: Why Maureen?

She worked in a dive bar for her tax-evader boss and served drinks to dope pushers, thieves, and murderers. This was too sophisticated to be any one of them. Was the case about him or was that also a decoy? Did someone think Maureen was important enough to cause a reaction but minor enough so as not to be considered family?

Chapter Eighteen

At the office of the Palmetto Pulse, Blu was escorted to the back by Josie. On the walk to Patricia's office, Blu said, "Your aunt tells me you're good at research."

Josie, young with chin length brown hair, glasses, and a professional but unrevealing pullover blouse and slacks, said, "I am. But I have to say, my aunt forbade me from working for you."

"Forbade?" he asked.

"Yeah. Something about getting shot at."

He nodded.

Before they got to the back office, Josie handed him a slip of paper. "Here's my email. Fifty an hour in cash if I find what you need."

Blu heard someone clear their throat and turned to see Patricia standing in her doorway.

She said, "I certainly hope you don't encourage my niece's delusion of working for you."

With a smile, Blu said, "Of course not," as he pocketed her email. "I'd never ask her to go to Southeast Asia in the middle of a war to cover underground CIA operations." This was exactly what Patricia had done in 1970 and how she'd met her future husband Reggie Sails. And she had done it at the age of twenty, which was most likely also Josie's current age.

"Good," Patricia said, ignoring Blu's jab.

Josie wisely kept her mouth shut, something that had taken Blu a lot longer than twenty years to control.

Patricia motioned for Blu to enter her office. Josie left them and returned to her desk.

On his drive over, Blu had received a call from Tess. Patricia had accepted an offer on the business.

Seated at her antique banker's desk, she asked, "How's Crome?"

Blu sat across from her in one of the two visitor's chairs. "I like him better when he works with me instead of against."

"Your partner strikes me as the independent type."

"Ya think?" Blu asked. "We spent way too much time tracking him down."

"You don't trust his judgment, do you?"

"Not in his current state of mind. Even when the job wasn't personal, he tended to push the limits. I don't want him to go off the deep end."

Josie carried in a tray holding a carafe and two mugs. "Coffee?"

She knew Patricia and Blu took theirs black, so no cream or sugar was required.

After setting the tray on the desk, filling the two cups, and handing them over, Josie left the room and closed the door.

"What's your next move?"

"I would like your niece to do some background on the list you gave me."

"I thought I just said I didn't want her to do any work for you."

"You did," he said. "She'd be working for you."

"And I'd want her to do this on my dime why, again?"

Blu held up his cup as a toast. "It'll be your last hurrah."

Patricia eyed him for a moment. "Good news travels fast."

"Think of the sources I have that you know about," he said still holding his cup up. "You trained them."

He, of course, was referring to Darcy Pelton, Harmony, and

Tess.

As if relenting, she met his toast.

They both drank what tasted to Blu like a good German roast.

"How are things with Billie?" she asked again.

The question, Blu assumed, was to let him know that just as he knew things about her, she also had sources. Probably the same sources.

"Not sure," he said.

"Give her some time," she said. "She's worth waiting for, if you're ready to settle down again."

Blu took another drink. He wasn't sure what he wanted anymore.

"Okay," Patricia said. "I'll have Josie look into the list."

After some more small talk and a promise for a game of horseshoes at his island home after this Maureen situation resolved itself, Blu made his way to the front door.

Passing the receptionist, Blu gave Josie a wave.

She held up a manila file. "Here."

"What's this?" he asked as he took the folder.

"Background on the list." She gave him a wink.

"Did you go rogue on this or were you given the task?"

Ignoring the question, she said, "Have a nice day!"

Wednesday, lunchtime

Tess met Blu at the Pirate's Cove and together they reviewed the work Josie had done.

Sitting at a table inside to avoid the ocean breeze blowing their papers everywhere, Tess said, "She does good work."

He had to agree.

"So how do you want to divide this?" she asked.

"Don't have to." Blu picked up his Atomic burger and took a bite.

"What?" she asked. "Am I supposed to read all this on my own?"

He chewed his food and washed it down with a Coke Zero, Tess' choice of drink. "If you want to. All I needed to do was scan them until I found what I was looking for."

With a smirk, she dipped her head and began reading.

While she read, he finished his lunch. When the last of the fries were gone, he sat back, wiped his mouth with a napkin, and watched her. It had been a year since she'd interviewed him in front of that burned out bait store off Folly Beach Road. He'd been working a job trying to find a spoiled brat named Jeremy Rhodes. Tess was the more business-minded of the duo that was her and Harmony. There'd been something between her and Blu, but nothing happened because Blu loved Billie.

Wednesday, mid-day

Crome drank from a cup of Starbucks and waited to see if his hunch would pan out. The hunch being that Maureen wasn't a decoy and something was at play that hadn't revealed itself yet. A long time ago, he learned from Blu that when things stopped making sense, the best course of action was to back up until they did. And what made sense was that Maureen had been taken to get at him. She had no enemies. He and Blu had lots of enemies. Actually, Crome knew his list was a lot longer than his business partner's. Either this was a local thing which was why it all happened to him, or someone had gone to great lengths to track him here. He ruled out everything other than local. He'd been back in Charleston for more than a year and the only new enemy they'd made—Sinclair Waters, a.k.a. Skull, crime lord of Columbia, South Carolina—was dead. Maybe someone from his organization or a relative was taking revenge. But the more he thought about it, the more Crome felt inclined to strike it from the list. The next man in line took over. He was probably more than happy about how things had turned out.

No. This had to be something else. This meant it had to be from the past. Not last year. But something older than four years, when he and Blu had been active in the area. Something before Crome's three-year sabbatical. And something that had left at least one person really pissed off.

He came up with a list of six previous clients, did some online searches, and crossed one off because he was dead. That left five names and he ranked them in order of how motivated they would be for revenge based on how the situations had played out. This was how he happened to be watching Clete Ramos from a corner table of the downtown Starbucks.

Even with Crome's admittedly limited online sleuthing skills (he was more of a leg-breaker type) he'd found Clete's current place of employment thanks to social media. Number one on the list, Clete lost everything when his wife at the time hired Blu Carraway Investigations to look into an odd charge on their credit card. A charge that Clete had told her was not legit. She'd agreed with him that it wasn't legit, but something had told the wiser-than-her-thirty-years woman her husband might not be telling the whole truth. Her instincts had been proven more right than she really wanted to deal with. Clete's sexual preferences had been yanked from the closet they'd been hiding in. And he'd lost his wife, his children, his job, and his relationship to his evangelical family. He'd gone from an up-and-coming executive at an investment firm to his current digs as a manager for a struggling retailer that pushed dollar wares to the general public. And, from what Crome could gather, he was losing a battle with booze.

Sitting by himself, Clete did a horrible job pretending not to scope out a table of teenage boys. It would have been nauseating to Crome if Clete had any game with them. But the middle-aged guy wasn't going to play ball any time soon with that group.

After a less than stellar attempt at an introduction followed quickly by a rude rebuff from the boys, Clete walked out.

Crome gave him ten paces, then got up and followed, throwing away his empty cup as he exited. His middle-aged and overweight target lumbered ahead toward a decade-old Nissan Sentra parked at a meter. Crome closed the distance just as Clete opened the driver's door.

Crome put a hand on the top edge of the door and pinned the man against his car. "Long time, Clete."

Clete stared at him wide-eyed at first, probably scared he was going to get robbed. And then his eyelids went back to normal and then his face bunched up as Crome caught a hint of recognition.

"You...you..." Clete began. "You're the one who ruined my life." He tried to force the door open.

Crome held firm. "You did that all by yourself when you lied to your wife."

Using his considerable mass, Clete managed to wedge himself in sideways.

Crome knew he wouldn't be able to hold the man forever. He let go of the door and backed away just as Clete attempted to push with all his might.

With nothing restricting the door from moving, it swung open fast, creaked against its hinges, and bent further than Nissan had designed it to, warping the sheet metal.

"Just checking in," Crome said. "Making sure you're still a jackass."

"Screw you, Crome. I'm gonna sue you for harassment."

Crome walked away, satisfied of two things. The first was that Clete was not the guy. The second was that Clete had no real case for harassment. That is, unless he wanted the video footage of him picking up male prostitutes handed over to the police.

Wednesday, mid-day, Pirate's Cove

Blu watched Tess look up from the list she'd been reading, the one Patricia had gotten and Josie had deciphered. Her serious look, the one that showed a slight worry line down the center of her forehead, was gone. In its place was a wide opened stare, the one she gave when she was surprised.

She said, "Does Crome know?"

"Not yet."

What she referred to was what Blu had seen. Someone had used Michael Crome's credit card to rent the room. The problem with this was that, as far as Blu's knowledge of his partner went, Crome didn't have any credit cards. If that were the case, then the man went to some length to get one in Crome's name. This wasn't the average kidnapper they were dealing with.

"So what do we do?" she asked.

Blu sat back. "Tell Crome, I guess."

"You guess?"

"I'm not sure he'll take it too well."

Tess' cell phone chimed and she looked at the display. "It's Harmony." She answered it and listened. Then to Blu she said, "You were right. Crome had a talk with Clete Ramos. He just left the man. According to Harmony, Crome gave him a good scare and walked away."

"He'll be checking on the second name on the list."

So far, Blu had been right. Crome's jab about not knowing what he'd be working on so Blu could work on something else had cut deep. After that, Blu got focused, came up with the list of names that appeared to be Crome's current playbook. He did know his partner's moves, he just didn't understand Crome's motive at first.

She said goodbye to Harmony and hung up.

"The tracker's working," Blu said. At least until Crome found out about it.

As if reading his mind, she said, "Until he finds it. Then he's really going to be pissed."

"I can handle him being pissed at me a lot better than him being pissed at the rest of the world."

*   *   *

The next name on the list for Crome was one Arthur Ryan. This one was another divorce case, but not quite as unorthodox as Clete's. They'd found Arthur bankrolling two mistresses. His wife didn't appreciate him sharing more than just her bed with the women. As far as Crome knew, Arthur was still paying his ex-wife. Her lawyer had gotten a very long alimony schedule that only stopped if she remarried. Crome had befriended her and spent more than a few nights over at Arthur's old mansion over the years. He'd laugh at the thought except Maureen's suffering wouldn't allow him any humor.

Arthur also turned out to be a dead end—his company had recently transferred him and his new family to Thailand. Crome started his bike and roared away.

On to number three.

Wednesday, mid-day

Harmony watched the blip from the tracker on Crome's motorcycle trace a route on the display of her iPad. This was much easier work than trying to tail someone. She'd been with both Blu and Crome when they'd attempted to do it the old-fashioned way and found it boring. And frustrating. This way she could trail far behind and not risk being spotted or losing Crome.

She didn't figure the older biker for a woman beater, but given his current state of mind, anything was possible. Based on that, it was probably for the best if Crome didn't know what she or Blu and Tess were up to. If he wanted to play this childish game, they'd let him as long as they could keep tabs on him.

And this way, she could stop at Starbucks for her venti-triple-skinny vanilla frappuccino.

Chapter Nineteen

Wednesday afternoon

While Tess dug into the history of Crome's credit card that paid for the room Maureen had been in when the picture was taken to see if there were any more expenses, Blu chased down another lead. This one wasn't so difficult and one that he should have thought of sooner. He placed a call, got voicemail, and left a message.

Andeline returned his call as he backed into a spot on King Street.

He answered with, "How's it going, And?"

"I'm fine. How's Crome?"

"What have you heard?" he asked, cutting to the chase.

"Someone sent him a picture of his woman with a gun to her head. Crome scared the crap out of Phineous and then bribed him with two really low-rent girls, if you ask me. And you're calling me. I'd say it's pretty serious."

"It is serious. Okay, so that's what you've heard. What do you know?"

She said, "Why don't you get out of your truck and come in so I can see that beautiful face of yours?"

Andeline was older than Blu by more than a decade and she enjoyed toying with him. She wasn't his type and never would be. But she was a fantastic source when he needed some obscure piece of information. Her contacts ran the gamut of the Charleston elite and underworld. Especially where those two worlds met up, which happened more than one would think. Money had a habit of causing the downfall of many a good man.

He did as she asked, got out of his truck, ignoring the meter since it was after six p.m. and walked into her restaurant. The former Madame in all senses of the title gave him a big grin when he walked in. Instead of their normal cursory banter and lack of physical touch, she stepped around her hostess podium, came over, gave him a tight hug, and a lingering peck on the cheek.

It occurred to Blu that Andeline might also be aware of his troubles with Billie.

They ended the embrace. Her bright blue eyes took him in and her dark hair with highlights that defied her age formed somewhat of a halo. She'd long ago stopped caring about what others thought of her weight, which Blu guessed measured over where the doctors said it should be. But she wore it well along with her designer dresses like the gray and white hugging number she had on at the moment.

She said, "I really wish you'd come around more than just when you need something."

"Me too, And, I mean it."

"Sure you do."

He looked down.

She said, "You eat dinner yet?"

The truth was he was starving and was planning on wolfing down three or four PB&J sandwiches at home later. "No."

Grabbing a menu, she said, "It appears I've got you right where I want you."

He wasn't sure what to say.

"Follow me." She led him to a vacant corner booth.

He sat and she said, "After I get someone to cover for me at the front, you and I are going to have a nice meal."

"Really, And, you don't have to go through all this trouble."

She leaned in close to him and held his chin in her hand. "I'm trying real hard to be a lady around you, Mr. Carraway."

With that, she stood upright and walked away, leaving Blu to contemplate how he'd gotten here. But he knew the answer. He was here to find information about Maureen's kidnapper. Andeline hadn't been this forward before. Something wasn't right. With a sudden urge to leave, he turned in his chair to get up but was stopped by Andeline now standing beside him.

"Going somewhere?" She placed a pint glass in front of him. Knowing, as all his friends did, that he didn't drink alcohol, she'd given him a dark soft drink. Bubbles in the glass floated to the top and quietly snapped and popped.

He raised his hands. "The restroom to wash up."

Giving him a knowing smile like she had caught him in a ruse, she waved her hand in the direction of the lavatories.

As he made his way to the restroom, he thought about the situation. Either this was a joke or she was serious. And there could only be one... no, two reasons why she'd be serious. The one he thought about immediately was she wanted to change their relationship from friendly to something else. The other was that she needed to talk to him about something important and was having a bit of fun at his expense. For the sake of sanity, he forced himself to think it was the latter. After he relieved himself and washed his hands, he walked out of the restroom with a better understanding of Andeline.

The first course of four—she-crab soup—along with Andeline awaited his return to the table. He seated himself, unfolded the napkin, picked up his spoon, and sampled the not-quite-bisque. It was perfect.

Andeline smiled at him.

He said, "This is one great restaurant you have here, And."

"I know." She spooned some soup.

"So what is it you want to tell me?"

"All business and no play makes Blu a dull boy."

Scraping the last bit of liquid off the bottom of the bowl, he said, "You know me too well."

"Yes, I do," she said. "And you are really rattled right now. Not because of me, not really. I'm sorry, I so enjoy taking advantage of your uncertainty."

"It's Crome," he said.

"I know."

He put down his spoon. "What else do you know?"

A waiter poured more wine into her glass and removed the empty soup bowls. She waited until he walked away. "I know about Maureen and that you two have been hunting her all over town. I know that your partner tried to go out on his own and you wouldn't let him. I know that no less than Patricia Voyels, Tess Ray and Harmony Childs, and Brack and Darcy Pelton are looking into it."

Their salads came.

After the waiter set the plates down, ground fresh black pepper over them, and left, Blu said, "What else?"

"None of my sources knows who is doing this."

Blu forked some ruffage. "That doesn't help me out here."

"It should," she said. "Think about it. If I don't know, it's not out there. You've gotten as far as I have, which is saying something, if you don't mind me saying."

"I don't, but I'm not happy about it."

"Happiness is a state of mind, my friend," she said. "I'm always happy because I choose to be."

He thought about countering her statement with something like, "Until someone sticks a gun to your head." But, as an ex-Madam who'd worked her way up from the bottom, Andeline had seen and experienced as much in her life has he had in his. Maybe more. That meant gunplay and death. This was nothing new to her. It was just another day.

The information he'd learned did not help him out, but he found himself beginning to relax.

And then she asked, "So how's Billie?"

Chapter Twenty

Wednesday, early evening

Harmony Childs knew she was playing a long shot. She'd come across something and decided to ditch tailing Crome and her normal nightly video post and go hunting for the jerk-wad who thought kidnapping a woman was okay.

Lucky for her, Tess had volunteered for "following Crome" duty tonight.

Harmony was still upset with Crome but this was about Maureen. No woman deserved to be going through what she was. This guy, if Harmony found him first, would experience hell on earth.

These were not normal thoughts for her, and she felt herself feeding on the anger stemming from her own morbidity.

Piloting her Jeep with the new tires Blu had bought after Crome shot out the back ones in order to save her, she cut off a tourist in a crossover SUV and merged onto Seventeen North toward Mount Pleasant. The transmission downshifted when she gave it the spurs and the two-ton off-road machine barreled up the incline and over the Cooper River.

The information that had caused her to take this detour from her normal life came in the form of an unsolicited call from one of her budding sources. The guy—they were mostly men—mentioned that he'd seen a man manhandle a woman out of the back of a van and into a pickup truck and speed away. This was not something that happened every day, she hoped. He'd described the woman as being attractive, tan, and Caucasian with tattoos on her arms and approximately forty years old. He'd described Maureen.

So Harmony had decided to take the bait.

Blu had told her not to go alone. Tess was busy following Crome who needed a padded room. There was no way in hell she was calling her old boss Patricia Voyels or her old nemesis Darcy Pelton. If somehow she could take Darcy's husband away from her, Harmony promised she'd be a good girl for the rest of her days. If Blu Carraway was a prettier Dos Equis commercial, Brack Pelton was Don Draper gift-wrapped in a suntanned beach bar owner.

Thinking about the men, and getting more than a tad worked up in the process, made her almost miss the turn.

Oh, yeah. There was a reason she was on this quest alone. She felt safe with her recently-purchased Ruger, Concealed Weapons Permit, and one-on-one tactical training by her recently-dumped S.W.A.T. boyfriend. The man had taught her a lot, but had no idea his time was limited to how much she felt she could learn from him. Most men in her life had been like that.

Unlike with that drug dealer who got the drop on her last year, she felt ready. No one would get the chance to shoot her again. If she'd learned anything from observing Blu and Brack and Crome, it was to shoot first and ask questions later. If someone drew down, she'd blow them away.

Another thing she'd learned from the men was to control the meeting location. Blu was particularly good at this and she'd observed him sidestep potential threats by stacking the deck in his favor.

She pulled in to the sand drive of the Pirate's Cove and parked.

Like Blu and Crome, Brack was an action junkie. She didn't exactly inform him of her intention to use his bar as a safe zone. God knew the place was anything but, given that it had already been shot up once in the past couple years. But the man knew how to defend himself and she'd personally seen the two pistols and shotgun kept close at hand behind the bar.

What she hadn't planned on, and now mentally kicked herself for, was her attire. This was a tourist town and she wore business casual. To everyone else around, she looked like someone who worked in an office celebrating happy-hour. It just so happened that the surroundings were a lowcountry island facing the Atlantic Ocean. Such was life in paradise.

She made her way up the front steps, opened the door, and cut through full tables of what she would guess were people from everywhere other than Charleston County eating plates of peel-and-eat shrimp and slurping margaritas. The place was booming, not just because of Brack's business manager's savvy management skills, but also because of his reputation of return fire.

The Isle of Palms Police Department had doubled in size thanks to him. With a positive spin on all the violence, the Town Council had reluctantly embraced the pirate image of the bar and used it to their advantage. It cost the council some overhead in the form of extra personnel, but the influx of tourists wanting to take selfies with the bullet holes purposely left in the walls more than made up for the additional expense.

Staffed almost entirely by single mothers, thanks to its sympathetic manager, the bar, like its owner, had a reputation. Except instead of one that skirted the law and could be prone to violence like Brack, the Pirate's Cove was known for the attractive wait staff and bartenders. The woman serving drinks behind the bar when Harmony walked up was an old acquaintance.

"How's it going, Harmony?" she said. "What'll you have?"

Dropping her purse on the left of two empty stools, Harmony pulled out the other and sat. "Hey, Valerie. I'll take a Corona and a menu."

Valerie got a bottle from the cooler, popped the top, and set it on a coaster in front of Harmony along with a slice of lime and the menu. She said she'd be back in a minute and went to serve other customers.

Harmony's use of the menu was mostly for cover. She had eaten in the place enough times that two of her suggestions had been added to it.

She ordered a grilled chicken sandwich with avocado called "the Harmony" and chips and salsa when Valerie returned.

While she waited for her food and her source, Harmony checked her phone and found two missed calls and a text. Her source was running late.

She was used to it. Half the time they never even showed up, so getting a courtesy message was a good sign that the meet would actually take place. As she set the phone on the bar next to her beer, she felt something poke her leg and looked down. It was Brack's dog, Shelby.

The beast wielded control over most women he came in contact with. Harmony knew she was no exception and didn't fight the urge to hop off her stool and squat to give him a proper greeting.

The dog licked her face and let her scratch him behind the ears. She might have entertained the thought about taking Brack home for a night, but she wanted Shelby forever.

A man's voice said, "Hey, Harmony."

Harmony looked up at Brack and said, "Hey, yourself."

"Business or pleasure?" he asked.

"That depends," she said. "What did you have in mind?"

If nothing else, the man was fun to toy with. Especially when she caught his suntanned face darken a shade.

"Very funny," he said. "I'll take that to mean you're working right now. Need me to stick around?"

"In more ways than one," she said.

He waited for her real answer.

She said, "I've got a source who says he might have seen Maureen. I hope you don't mind the information exchange taking place here."

He said, "Not at all."

Backup sufficiently secured, Harmony got to her seat, squeezed the lime in her beer, and took a long pull. Eventually, she wanted to be in a bigger city covering bigger things. But when this situation was resolved, it would be the story in the lowcountry. At least, she planned on making it so, but only after Maureen was returned home safely and the kidnapper sufficiently dead.

Chapter Twenty-One

Wednesday, early evening

The man watched Harmony sitting at the bar flirting with the owner and his dog. He sure seemed interested in her.

Women were just users and teases. Harmony was youthful but nowhere near innocent. He knew because he'd been following her for the past few nights—ever since that blowup in McDonalds where she told Crome off. He felt she was someone he should get to know. So he put a tracker on her car and watched her when time allowed.

The woman had three different guys she was seeing. Or sleeping with. She was no different than any other woman he'd come across lately. Except for Maureen, who as far as the man could tell, stayed truer to Crome than he did to her. He knew the time was right after the night Crome stayed out with Ms. Harmony sitting over there and her cohort, Tess. They'd drank together first at a bar downtown, and then back at Harmony's apartment two blocks away. Meanwhile, Maureen's car, he knew because he'd also had a tracker on it, had been at home the whole time waiting on Crome to return. The biker was such an ass.

The man would show her he was better for her than Crome. That would put her biker boyfriend over the edge. He'd already showed her he was more faithful than Crome simply by returning every night to rub lotion on her back. Sooner or later, she'd let him do it without shackles and medication, but these things took time.

Harmony had already wreaked enough havoc with Maureen's and Crome's relationship. Maureen might just appreciate the gesture if something bad were to happen to the young woman.

As he finished the thought, the mutt Harmony played with on the floor jumped up, looked in his direction, and bared his teeth as if reading his mind.

Smart dog.

While he loved most animals, he hated dogs. Here was another reason why.

Harmony nursed a second beer, hope of the source showing up dwindling with every sip. Every time her phone chirped, she'd look at the display. Normally she liked it when her men messaged her. But now they were just false positives. She didn't want to hear from them. She wanted to hear from the source who seemed to be playing a pathetic game.

The conversation with Brack, while deliciously playful, had turned business when he asked if she wanted him to shoot to kill. From just about anyone else, that line would be nothing but a bad joke, or at least one in poor taste. From Brack, it was serious. He took things to the edge and then jumped off.

Her instruction had been to incapacitate but not fatally wound. They still hadn't found Maureen. A dead source or kidnapper told no tales.

The next phone chirp was Tess. Thinner by ounces, Tess had the true light blonde hair men sometimes killed for, and that glasses-wearing librarian thing going for her. The problem as Harmony saw it was that Tess was too damn smart for her own good. She had no heart, at least not one that got in the way of advancing her career. While Harmony always had at least two, or sometimes three like at present, men to toy with, Tess struggled to hold onto one. They'd be attracted to her physical beauty but most couldn't hold an intelligent conversation to keep her attention.

Harmony's strength, as she saw it, was reading people, seeing what they had to offer, and getting what she could from them. Tess didn't have the patience.

The mistake Harmony knew she'd made last year, when she got in her Jeep with Tim the drug dealer and thinking it was a good idea, was pride. Crome, whom she'd been toying with, had broken protocol and asked Brack to find out from Darcy some information. Nothing wrong except that sooner or later, Harmony would have found it. But the man had gone around her. And no one went around Harmony, as far as she was concerned.

So she got shot for being a bonehead. She wouldn't make that mistake again. Brack's wife might not appreciate Harmony using her husband as backup, but that didn't stop him from agreeing so it must be okay, right?

Someone like Tess would dismiss the whole idea as illogical, but Harmony knew deep down that she used people. She was using Brack. After being shot, she had done a lot of self evaluation and had decided from then on to be honest with herself no matter what.

People like Brack could die helping her. She knew this. Such was life.

Wednesday, early evening

Volunteering to monitor the tracker they'd placed on Crome's motorcycle, Tess decided, was not the most rewarding of tasks. But it had to be done. The man was out of control, but only inasmuch as he was dissing his friends and she couldn't understand why.

With a borrowed Toyota Camry and the tablet from Harmony, Tess had done her best to keep up with the biker. It wasn't easy. The man must have thought obeying traffic laws was a voluntary activity. The poor car gave all she had, and it was barely enough at times. Luckily the tracker made up the difference. If she lost him, and it happened quite frequently, the tracker told her by how far.

Crome must have sensed he was being followed because he

doubled back several times, making extra turns. He'd almost outsmarted her on more than one occasion, and once to the point that the cover of her rolling incognito car would be blown. She'd had to pull into a gas station and duck when he'd made a quick U-turn and accelerated back toward her. Lucky for her, the sound of his straight-piped exhaust announced both his presence and departure. She'd simply waited for the rumble to lessen.

What she didn't expect was his destination. When he turned into the parking lot of the Palmetto Pulse, she nearly followed behind him, catching herself at the last minute and accelerating away.

Parking a block down with a view of the exit of the lot, she put on a baseball cap and called Harmony. Together they'd decide if they were ready to call Blu yet.

Chapter Twenty-Two

Wednesday, early evening

The office of the Palmetto Pulse was neat and tidy, if getting sparser the closer it came to the date of sale. Through multiple sources, Crome had learned that Patricia's decision to sell was not received well by most of the locals. Her paper was one of the few in the region that printed the news straight with no slant, political party or otherwise. Given Patricia's propensity to document her nephew's escapades as well as the most recent Blu Carraway Investigations job that ended badly for more than a few people, it wasn't hard for her to toe the line and keep her reputation intact.

A cute young girl sat behind the receptionist desk. Crome had met her before—Patricia's great niece if he remembered right.

"Hey, Mr. Crome," she said.

"Hey, there," he read the name on the plate in front of her, "Josie."

She grinned, catching his forgetting her name. "Would you like me to see if my aunt is available?"

"I could walk back there and find out myself," he said.

"No," she said, with another smile, "you can't. Or she'll be mad at me."

"She's your aunt. I think she'd get over it."

"Why risk it?" The young woman stood and motioned toward the chairs in the corner. "Have a seat and I'll let her know you're here."

He nodded and took a seat, thinking she was all right.

What seemed like less than thirty seconds passed and then Josie was back, along with her great aunt.

Patricia leaned against her niece's desk. "You're a tough man to figure out."

Standing, Crome said, "That's the way I like it."

With the crook of a finger, she motioned for him to follow her.

And he found himself thinking not exactly wholesome thoughts about the strong businesswoman in front of him as he trailed her into the back offices of her soon-to-be-sold empire.

In her office, with the door remaining open, she sat behind a large, banker's desk. Crome sat in one of the visitor's chairs facing her, relinquishing some of the power of the conversation to her by the seating arrangement. On the desk were what looked like trinkets she'd collected over the years. Framed plaques of various awards hung on the walls around the room.

He said, "I appreciate you seeing me."

Sitting straight in her chair, she said, "Of course. What is it you'd like to talk about?"

"The information you gave Blu."

"What do you think I gave him?"

"Something better than I had."

She leaned forward. "Why do you think that?"

He smelled her perfume, Chanel No. 5 if he had to guess. "Because he let me go without much of a fight."

"I was told you threw him between two tables in the McDonald's."

That made him smile. She already knew what went down. Anyone who thought money was power didn't understand how much control having the right information wielded. Patricia had a lot of money, that was fact. But she had enough information on everyone of importance in this town to make J. Edgar Hoover jealous. She just didn't use it like he did.

He said, "He let me get away a little too easy."

"You don't think you beat him to the punch, so to speak?"

Shaking his head, he said, "Naw. I've known him too long. No one beats Blu Carraway to the punch."

"Then you're smarter than you look."

"I've been told that before. It's called tradecraft."

"So is knowing when to go rogue and when not to."

He sat back and propped a foot up on his knee. "You think I don't know what I'm doing?"

"I think you think you're being so smart. All you're doing is making your friends work extra hard while Maureen is in the hands of some monster."

That barb stuck in deep, going through his heart and out his back, a big mother of a boar spear with hook points and serrations and a two-foot-long tip. And it caused quite a bit of spit and vinegar to seep out the exit wound.

Much like the phone call with Harmony, he'd just been skewered by Patricia. At least this time it was in a semi-private setting.

He said, "So are you going to tell me what you gave him or what?"

She folded her arms across her chest. "I'm going with 'or what.'"

Her defiance was almost too much to bear. It made him want to stand up and shove all her neat trinkets off her antique desk. But he resisted the urge.

"What do I have to do to get you to help me?"

"Work with your partner. And your friends."

"I didn't think I had any friends left."

She raised herself out of her chair and walked around the desk to him.

He stood and faced her.

Wrapping her arms around him in a gesture that caught him off guard, she said, "You do. I'm a friend. So are Harmony and Tess. And Darcy and my nephew. And so is Blu."

He didn't see this coming, her taking on a comforting role. He said, "I'm here, ain't I?"

"You are," she said, unwrapping her arms and looking at him. "But we're all a package deal."

Wednesday, early evening

Blu Carraway sat in the passenger seat of Tess's borrowed Camry and watched his partner roar away from the office of the Palmetto Pulse.

Tess said, "Wonder what they talked about."

Getting out of the car, Blu leaned back in and looked at the woman too smart to understand how distracting her beauty could be.

"What?" she asked.

"Stay on Crome. I'll call you later."

"I've heard that before."

He walked across the street and entered the Palmetto Pulse. Josie was behind the receptionist desk.

"Hey, Mr. Carraway. I'll let Patricia know you're here."

He felt himself smile. "Thanks, Josie. And call me Blu."

Her calling him Mr. Carraway made him feel older than his forty-five years.

She got up, all of twenty years old, suntanned and toned from training for beach volleyball competitions. He had to remind himself, again, that he was too old and should be focused on the task at hand and not how she looked in her skirt. It was just that it had been a while since he'd been with Billie, her leaving town and all.

Patricia didn't help matters much except he didn't feel as guilty about their mutual attraction. She was old enough to know better. Standing beside the desk as Josie returned to her seat and the ringing phone, Patricia said, "It seems like I just did this with your partner."

"I saw him leave."

"And you want to know what we talked about."

"Not really," Blu said.

"Something we need to discuss in my office, I presume?" she asked.

"Who else is here?"

"You mean besides me and Josie? No one."

"Then we can chat right here. Probably better for all parties concerned."

Patricia gave him what amounted to a combination of a frown and a smile.

He said, "I've got my partner under surveillance."

"I figured as much," she said. "I also get the feeling he knows although he hasn't found the tracking device yet."

"Which is why I'm here."

She folded her arms across her chest. "I'm listening."

"I might need your wizard niece here to commit a felony."

"No chance."

Josie hung up the phone. "What would be the charge?"

"I'm not exactly sure."

"Wow!" Josie said. "Color me interested."

Patricia said, "The answer is still no."

"As soon as Crome finds the tracker Tess's friend stuck on the inside fender of his bike, he'll disappear."

With a snap of her fingers, Josie said, "You want me to track him by his phone."

"Yes."

With more emphasis, Patricia said, "Absolutely not."

Josie said, "I'll see what I can do."

Patricia looked at both of them as if they had lost their minds. "Am I speaking to the walls?"

"No," Blu said. "You're not. I'd ask my police contacts but they have too much oversight and frown on requests like this. Besides, Crome wouldn't appreciate if I sent them after him. They already have a love-hate thing going on."

"You mean they love to hate him?" Patricia asked.

"That about sums it up."

"Why don't I just ask my nephew to sit on him for you?"

Blu said, "I thought about that but your nephew's skills lie elsewhere. He'd probably do it, but I don't want any bad blood between him and Crome." Brack would come in handier after the kidnapper was cornered and the guns came out.

"What's Crome's cell number?" Josie asked, already typing on her laptop.

"Didn't you hear what I said?" Patricia said. "The answer is no. Especially from my computer in my office."

"I thought you signed the papers," Blu said.

She looked at him. "I did, but it's still mine until the end of the month."

Josie, still typing, said, "My laptop."

"My wifi," Patricia snapped back.

Typing fingers stopped. Josie gave her aunt a look that would have scared Blu if he'd received it. She closed the laptop with a loud click, stood, and put it in her backpack. "I'm calling it a day." With that, she slung the backpack on a shoulder and walked out.

Patricia said, "Do you see what you're doing?"

"She's more like you than you want to admit."

"And if she goes to jail, what are we going to do then?"

"Bail her out and put her on my payroll."

All pleasantries gone, Patricia got in Blu's face. "You better be thankful that Josie is as good at hacking as she is. Otherwise, she would get caught. And I'd have to shoot you."

Not wanting to taunt the lioness any more than he'd already done, he said, "I believe you."

"Now if you'll excuse me, I have a business dinner with the mayor that I need to get ready for." She stepped back, gave him a curt smile, and walked back to her office.

All that was left of her presence was the scent of Chanel No. 5.

Thinking back, as he stood there, he couldn't recall another time where someone had gotten in his face and didn't suffer for it. He supposed there was a first time for everything.

As he exited the office, he spun the open sign hanging in the window to closed and walked back to his truck.

The Fixx's "One Thing Leads To Another" began when he turned the key.

Wednesday, eleven p.m.

Harmony had another source to check out. Unlike the one that was supposed to meet her at the bar, this one would most likely not stand her up. He'd called and almost sounded desperate. The poor man wanted attention. And that's what she'd give him, as long as he was useful.

The only problem she saw was that it wasn't related to Maureen's kidnapping. It was another story she'd been working on. There were pangs of guilt, but she didn't think taking an hour or two to work on something else would hurt anything. It might give her enough distance from the problem to have a much-needed breakthrough.

Chapter Twenty-Three

Thursday
DAY FOUR

The four a.m. call woke everyone up. Maybe it wasn't everyone all at once, but within fifteen minutes of the first call to the last, they were all awake. It started with a call to Darcy Pelton from an old source who still fed her information even though she wasn't in the business any more. The subject of the call was that the mayor had gone missing at sea. Radio contact with him had failed and the Coast Guard was looking for his boat.

More out of loyalty than anything else, Darcy called Patricia. Patricia in turn, and for reasons she really didn't want to think too hard about, what with a two-wine-bottle hangover from her business dinner that ended badly, called Blu Carraway. Blu called Crome. Then he called Tess.

The call to Darcy started the chain reaction. It was the call Blu made to Crome and Crome's response that triggered the gathering. And the panic.

They all agreed to meet at the Pelton home on Sullivan's Island. It was the only place large enough to accommodate them easily and still be close to the action.

Blu Carraway arrived late. Most times living forty-five minutes south of Charleston was a blessing, what with the influx of new inhabitants and his penchant for peace and quiet. Forty-five minutes south of Charleston made it an hour and change to Sullivan's Island.

The Peltons' home was ocean front and, no doubt thanks to Darcy, well appointed. That wasn't a shot at Brack's wealth status sans his wife. Pelton had enough fundage coming in from his two restaurants to afford to purchase, and subsequently lose in a fiery explosion, a new Porsche 911 convertible covered only by liability insurance. He was well off in most anyone's book.

Already parked on the artisan brick drive when Blu pulled in were Patrcia's Mercedes and Tess's convertible Beetle. Two of the four garage doors were open and exposed Pelton's black Mustang and his wife's new Grand Cherokee.

The first thing that came to Blu's mind was this was a meeting of one percenters and he, Crome, and Tess were merely guests. Money, Blu had come to realize, didn't buy happiness. But, as the country song by Chris Janson went, it could buy boats and nice trucks to pull them. And beach front homes and information.

He got out of his three-year-old Nissan Xterra, a truck he considered a luxury because it was still new to him and had working air conditioning and satellite radio tuned in to the eighties alternative station.

The home, elevated due to building codes established after Hurricane Hugo put Charleston under ten feet of water for a week, had two sets of stairs, one on each side, leading to the oversized front porch. The stairs and the porch were sanded and stained a light brown, bucking the Charleston trend of everything being pastel and trimmed in white.

Before he could get to the top of the stairs, Blu was greeted by Shelby. The dog had been instrumental in rescuing Hope from a nasty abductor. Blu had tried to reward Shelby with treats but he only ate food from Brack, Darcy, and a woman who watched him from time to time named Trish Connors. Considering the world today, Blu thought the dog wise beyond his years.

Pelton stood at the top of the stairs holding two cups of coffee.

He had been a train wreck when Blu first met him. At the time, Darcy lived in Atlanta and was with another man and Pelton did not take it well. Now, with Darcy as Pelton's wife, it was as if he had turned a corner in his life.

Pelton said, "It's about time you got here. Ever thought of moving closer to civilization?"

From a stooped position on the stairs, Blu continued to give Shelby a good scratch behind the ears. "Why would I want to do that?"

"Good question. Coffee?"

"Please." Blu stood and Shelby escorted him up the stairs.

The two men and Shelby stood on the front porch enjoying the coolness of the early morning. Blu caught more than a hint of bug spray emitting from Pelton. On the island and so close to the marsh, mosquitoes and no-see-ums were a staple.

Blu may have arrived late, but apparently he wasn't last. The chugga chugga roar patented by Harley Davidson started as a low rumble and grew louder as it approached. He and Pelton watched Crome idle onto the drive, make a lazy loop behind the parked vehicles, and drop the kickstand beside Blu's truck.

Apparently Blu would not have to take Josie up on her offer to track the biker by his phone. At least as long as he continued to show up upon request.

Shelby bounded down the steps again and greeted the biker.

Crome stooped to pet the dog.

"Got more coffee inside," Pelton said. "Darcy made breakfast. Come on in."

After Crome topped the stairs, with Shelby in the lead, they all went inside. Patricia, Tess, and Darcy stood around the center island in the kitchen. Sitting out, buffet style, were a mostly eaten quiche and a second whole one, a bowl of cut fruit, and a plate of scones.

Crome reached inside his vest, pulled out a small black device and handed it to Tess. "I think this might be yours."

It was the tracker they'd installed on his motorcycle.

Tess gave him a weak smile. "If you hadn't turned into such an ass, we wouldn't have needed it."

Pelton stepped between them and handed Crome a cup of coffee.

Crome said, "Harmony was with the mayor last night."

Blu hadn't mentioned to the group exactly why they should meet, just that they needed to. After the call from Blu, Tess had tried to contact Harmony and only got voicemail.

Patricia stammered, "How...when...it couldn't be..."

Continuing, Crome said, "We're all friends here, right?"

Not exactly an appropriate question from him at the moment, Blu thought, considering the exercise he'd just put them through.

Crome said, "I was following Harmony to make sure she was safe. It seemed to me she could be the next most likely one in trouble. She met the mayor at the marina and they went out on his boat."

Tess said, "And now they're both missing."

Crome said, "I hope I'm not right about this."

"Could be," Pelton said, "that the Coast Guard will find them come first light."

Tess said, "It doesn't feel like it's going to go that way to me."

Darcy put an arm around Tess.

"Harmony must have kept this a secret." Tess looked at Patricia. "I didn't know, and I normally know everything she's up to."

"Well, she wasn't the first woman he took out there on his boat," Patricia said, no emotion in her voice.

Nobody in the room dared ask if she'd been one as well. Blu suspected she hadn't.

Darcy said, "We've got two missing women. Might be connected. Might not. Either way, our work just doubled."

Blu watched the group react to what she'd said. Patricia was probably contemplating the fact that it could have been her instead of Harmony. Tess showed real concern for her BFF. Darcy had already kicked into business mode. Blu was surprised Brack wasn't cleaning his guns in preparation for a fight. Crome leaned against the doorway, actually sipping a cup of coffee, appearing to take in the scene.

Chapter Twenty-Four

Tess drove into the city, the top down on her convertible Volkswagen and the sun warming her face and exposed shoulders. Traffic across the Cooper River Bridge was steady but just past rush hour crazy.

She'd known something was wrong. Felt it. It was like that with her and Harmony.

Harmony had been acting different lately and Tess knew she was hiding something. Having an affair with the married mayor wasn't in and of itself something worth hiding. Tess had a feeling it was less about romance, if at all, and more about some lead. Harmony had no problem using her sexuality to get what she needed. This was much like Darcy Pelton using her family money to buy information—whatever it took to get to the truth of the story.

A long time ago, Tess had drawn lines for herself that she never crossed. She never slept with a man for any reason besides love or basic attraction. She never paid too much money for information. She always kept her sources confidential. And she obeyed her conscience. Because of these lines, she never felt the need to hide things from Harmony. There was nothing to hide.

She parked in the downtown marina, the same place where four years ago a Charleston Police Detective had gunned down a local mobster named Michael Galston. Brack, Darcy, and Patricia Voyels had also been involved. It had been related to the murder of

Brack's uncle and Patricia's ex-husband.

The man working the office at the marina, an older gentleman with white hair and a growing bald patch on the back of his head, a Jimmy Buffet T-shirt, cargo shorts, and flip flops greeted her.

She showed him her press credentials. "Tess Ray, investigative reporter."

Donning reader glasses, the man said, "That's what it says. What can I do for you, Ms. Ray?" He grinned as he looked her up and down.

Was he flirting with her? Her instinct said yes.

"And you are?" she asked, not exactly shutting him down, but not giving him anything either.

"Jack Rube. I'm the manager."

"What kind of security do you have here, Mr. Rube?"

"Call me Jack," he said. "During the day, you got me. I'm free most nights."

Ignoring the obvious ploy, she asked, "Does someone else watch the slips at night?"

"Sure. Plus we got a really good camera system. Me and the owners can access it twenty-four seven."

"You don't happen to keep digital records, do you?"

He smiled. "We do."

"Is it possible to view the footage from last night?"

Another smile. "It is."

"Can I?"

The smile left. "I'm afraid I can't share it with you. If you tell me what this is about, maybe I can take a look for you."

If she mentioned that the mayor was missing, he would probably clam up and wait for the police to come in with a warrant. She needed to see it now.

"A friend of mine who I suspect is missing might have gotten on a boat last night."

"You mean Harmony?"

Sometimes her reputation preceded her. This guy had her pegged before she flashed him her credentials.

"Yes."

"You jealous or something?"

"Not jealous. Concerned."

He opened his hands. "Now how am I supposed to know that?"

"She and I are like sisters. We always keep in touch."

"Not in this case," he said.

"I'm not concerned with whose boat she got on," Tess said. "I already know which one."

"Then what are you asking?"

"I need to know if anyone else besides her and the owner got on the boat."

The man visibly stiffened. "Is something going on?"

That was the money question. "I'm not sure."

"Will the police be coming by asking the same questions?"

She couldn't lie. "Probably."

"Then I need to wait for them."

Tess never put herself in a position of weakness. Meaning, she always did her homework. This guy, this Jack Rube, underestimated her. Most men did.

She pulled her phone out. "I'll be happy to call them."

He smiled, a big stupid grin, as if he were trying to call her bluff.

"They'll want to see the footage from the cameras."

"Like you said," he replied.

"All of the cameras."

His grin was still there, but it began to wane.

It was Tess's time to smile. "I'm talking all the footage from the last month."

Not only did his grin fade away, but an uncomfortable smirk replaced it.

"Now if I were managing this place and knew some characters were running bricks of pot through here and the police had me on video with them, I might get nervous."

Jack Rube finally broke his own silence. "You're playing a dangerous game, you know?"

"What I know," Tess said, "is that my friends and I are several steps ahead of the police. I know that because I'm here and they aren't. Yet."

"I think it's time for you to leave." His suntanned face had grown a few shades darker.

"The smart play here, because I'm guessing the footage is all on file with a backup in the Cloud, is to let me see it."

"I don't see how that's in my best interest," he said.

Because you don't have a lot of vision, she thought. "Because you aren't looking at the big picture."

"Which is?" He had a glimmer of hope in his eyes.

"If we find Harmony before the detectives on the case figure out about your camera system, they may not even come by."

"So," he said, almost thinking to himself, "I'd be helping you find her? And the mayor?"

"Exactly," she said. "His boat didn't return, did it?"

Jack Rube looked toward a row of slips and said, "No, it didn't." He scratched his two-day-old whiskers that were as white as his hair.

She could picture him wanting to spark up a bong "to help him think this through."

After what seemed like more than fifteen seconds, he said, "Okay. I'll let you see them."

She handed him a jump drive from her purse. "Can you put it on this?"

"How much do you want?"

"Last twenty-four hours."

"You're crazy. And you got a death wish. If you know so much then you know the others on the film won't want anyone seeing them, much less the press."

"It's me or the cops, Jack. Time to fish or cut bait."

He took the jump drive, rolled it between his fingers. "How about this and dinner?"

"How about the files and you won't see me again?"

The grin was back. "Fair enough. But the deal is no one knows what you got or who you got it from."

"Agreed."

After thirty minutes of Jack simultaneously copying files and gaping at her legs and breasts, she was out of there.

What a slime ball. But, he actually bought her story. Of course, if he ever got wise, he might let his drug dealer friends know she had them on film. It would most likely mean his own death sentence, but he didn't seem bright to begin with.

Chapter Twenty-Five

Thursday, eleven a.m.

Rod Stewart's "If You Think I'm Sexy" blared on an old radio in the corner of the rundown vape store when Crome entered. He'd run through the vape juice he had with him in the saddle bags of his bike and the ones he'd stashed, in case of emergency, in his beach rental and needed more—a lot more.

The woman behind the counter had a short and round shape with tattoos recently added to pale, white skin. What she needed, and Crome knew he was too far gone because he was wasting brain cells thinking about this seriously, was an hour walk each day in the sunshine.

She handed him his nicotine and a new flavor, caramel. It was Maureen's favorite. He paid and left the store, now thinking he was glad he hadn't relapsed and stopped at the corner for a bag of reds. Speed certainly tuned him up and sharpened his edge into a lethal blade. Part of him was busy trying to convince the other part that he could use the bump.

The rest of him still remembered the weekend he went cold turkey—a living hell that lasted a month. Plus, he liked stockpiling money these days. At his peak of drug use, the red habit ate up five hundred a week. That was ten years ago. God only knew how much the stuff cost now.

When he'd quit, one of his dealers had made the mistake of coming around trying to get him to relapse. Crome taught the man a lesson, and the dealer, his name was Fred, had walked around with a cast on his arm for six weeks. Everyone in the life had known what happened, and no other dealers approached him after that.

His cell phone buzzed as he mounted his bike. He looked at the display, saw Tess's number and answered.

"Yo."

She said, "You up for watching some home movies?"

"Of you?"

"The marina."

The power of a beautiful woman. He and Blu would have had to break in and steal the footage. Tess just walked in and asked for it. The wonders never ceased.

He said, "Your place or mine?"

"Yours," she said. "That way I can leave if you irritate me."

"Fair enough. You want me to stop and pick up Chinese?"

Chinese? Jesus, he really had to get his head screwed back on straight. Right after he took another hit from his jacked-up vaporizer.

He did.

Much better.

"Actually," she said, "that would be great. See you in about half an hour."

Forty minutes later, after he'd stopped and purchased two bags full of stir-fry, wonton soup, and egg rolls and had them sitting on his kitchen counter, Tess walked in. She had a tote bag slung over a shoulder exposed thanks to the tank top she wore and carried a six pack of Coke Zero.

"Kinda defeats the purpose, don't you think?" he asked.

She set her purse and the drinks on his recently wiped off kitchen table. "What does?"

He watched her slide the backpack off. "The whole diet drink thing." Pointing at the food, he said, "There's about a million calories right there and only two of us."

"I've got a date with my personal trainer in four hours," she said. "That should burn off most of lunch. What're you gonna do?"

He put his hands behind his head and kicked back. "Oh, I don't know. Take a run down the beach later."

"Yeah, right. I remember you saying you never ran."

"Especially if someone was chasing me."

"Ha."

She set the backpack and purse on his table and opened the fridge. "I was expecting your refrigerator to need a good cleaning. But it looks like all you put in here is beer."

"What else do I need?"

She pulled a Coke off the six pack, set the rest of them on a shelf and shut the fridge door. "Oh, I don't know. How about food?"

"Don't cook."

It looked like she was going to say something else and then stopped herself. Probably, he thought, a wise move.

Twisting the top of her bottle of Coke, she said, "I'll get the computer connected to your TV. Why don't you get the food out? You got plates?"

Crome pulled a package of Styrofoam plates and bowls from a second bag and set them on the table.

"Good enough." She gave him a smile and went on taking wires and electronic devices out of her backpack.

While she did that, he took out the containers, opened them up, and stuck plastic forks in the food. He then put the packs of soy sauce, hot mustard, and duck sauce in a pile.

"You want me to fix you a plate?" he asked.

She was in the middle of connecting some wires to the jacks in the TV and turned her head to look at him.

He wasn't sure what to make of this. She looked great, like always. Those librarian glasses on her nose.

"What?" he asked.

"Um," she said, "sure." She turned back to her work.

He poured soup in the bowls, put an egg roll on each plate, added brown rice and topped the rice off with three small piles of the dishes he'd purchased. The plates had equal amounts of food. He didn't eat often, but when he did, he ate a lot.

Carrying the full plates first, he set them on the coffee table in front of the couch that faced the TV. On the second trip, he had the soup and utensils. A third was needed for the condiments and his own Coke.

She completed all the connections about the same time he'd finished getting the meal ready. Everything she'd done with the wires was like a foreign language to him.

"Where's the TV remote?" she asked.

He got up, found it stuck between the cushions of the couch, and handed it to her. Not big on TV, the last time he remembered turning it on was to watch the national dirt bike championship. That was a few weeks ago, well before Maureen got taken.

Tess pushed some buttons and a source menu came up on the screen. She selected an input and then her laptop display also showed up on his TV. She went back to her laptop, moved the mouse and got something running. The display on both monitors changed to a scene on the water. The downtown marina on the Ashley River. He recognized it because he'd been there the night before—wooden decking with rows and rows of slips for different size boats.

He dipped his egg roll in a puddle of mustard and crunched down on it.

She sat beside him, picked up the bowl, held it close to her mouth, and spooned some soup. "I loaded it from a couple hours before the last time I spoke with Harmony."

Sitting next to him, the two of them alone in his house, he realized how much of a dirt bag he'd been to both her and Harmony and Blu and Patricia. Of course he'd never admit it aloud.

Her spoon in mid-flight to her mouth, she paused. "What?"

"Huh?"

"You're looking at me, but not like you're checking me out like you usually do."

"Huh?" He couldn't think of anything else to say and didn't want to spout out the truth.

"Never mind." She slurped her soup in the most ladylike

manner he'd ever seen.

She said, "There it is again."

"Are we gonna watch the video or not?" he asked, now a little uncomfortable. First Harmony chewed him out, now Tess was reading his mind. He really needed to get away again. Maybe after this was over, after he killed whoever had Maureen, he'd leave town. Get back down to the degenerate side of Key West. Drown in margaritas and señoritas for a few months, try and forget everything.

"There he is," she said.

Crome kicked out of introspection and focused on the TV. The image had gone from dusk to dark and the lights perched over the slips illuminated the dock. A man walked down the wood planks toward a small yacht. It took a few moments for Crome to recognize him.

"I still can't believe she bopped the mayor," he said.

With more than a hint of coolness in her voice, Tess said, "We don't know what they were doing."

"If that boat leaves the dock and heads out to sea with her on it, there's only a few reasons to go through all this trouble."

"Is that all you ever think about?"

"Yep."

"Figures."

The man hopped onto the boat and swung himself to the console. Soon after, the boat lights turned on and the mayor could clearly be seen fiddling with the controls.

"Probably checking the fuel level," Crome said. "You know, he was a client of ours a while back. What a tool."

"Should we be looking at him?" she asked.

"I doubt it," Crome said. "It was a private security job and he's still living."

Another figure appeared. It was Harmony.

Tess let out a slight gasp.

"Gotta be some angle she's playin' here," Crome said. At least he hoped so. Anything else would be, well, he wasn't sure what that would be. There was every bit of thirty-plus years between their ages.

They both watched Harmony, wearing a tank top and short skirt, board the boat with the help of the mayor. He then untied the lines and started the motor and they left the slip.

"We've got to go earlier to see if anyone besides the two of them got on that boat," he said.

"You're assuming the mayor isn't our dirt bag."

"Oh," Crome said, "he's a dirt bag, all right. But I'm pretty sure he's not the kidnapping kind. Want some coffee?"

She held up her bottle of soda. "I'm good."

Crome went to his kitchen, dumped out the old grinds and filter, and reloaded it, adding enough water for a full pot.

Tess said, "You're not drinking?"

It came out with equal parts surprise, apprehension, concern, and approval.

He looked over at her. "I'm not popping amphetamines either if that helps you."

"It doesn't."

She was one sharp cookie. Probably smarter than him and Blu if he had to guess. He knew what she meant. It wasn't a secret to him that he was a functioning addict. Just because he'd been able to wean himself off of the red pills didn't mean he was clean. Every day for him until Maureen's disappearance consisted of drinking at least a six pack. Now even the booze was on the back burner. He'd hate to see his blood-nicotine level, though.

"What would?" he asked.

"What would what?"

"Help you?"

Straightening her back, she looked directly at him. "What would help me is for you to not go off again and try to solve this yourself."

"I thought we'd moved past that," Crome said.

"Frankly," she said, "I only have to put up with you for as long as I care to. But Blu is your business partner. And he's your friend.

You tried to screw him over."

"Blu plays by too many rules."

"Not so sure I agree with you on that one," she said.

Where was this going? He had no idea.

"Did you find a new place for us to watch on the video?"

"Don't like the topic of conversation?"

"Something like that," he said, not sure what else to say.

She gave him a grin, but he knew it wasn't from happiness. Her friend was in trouble and she was taking out some frustration on him. That was okay. He deserved her words. She was a good kid.

"Yeah," she said. "I'm ready when you are."

The coffee pot beeped. He rinsed his mug out, ignoring the dark rings coloring the inside of it, the ones keeping track of the days since it had been washed properly, and filled the cup.

He seated himself next to her again and she pressed play. They watched the comings and goings of people in the marina. After a while, Crome could pick out who worked there by what they were doing on the screen.

Crome saw something and said, "Hold it."

Tess paused the video.

"Back it up thirty seconds," Crome said.

She did.

There it was. A man strolled down the dock, passed the mayor's boat, and then slipped back on from the stern. It was a smooth move and not one most people would have picked up on.

She replayed it in slow motion and paused at the best shot at the man's face. It was grainy, but Crome could tell he was in his fifties, well-toned, and agile enough.

Tess said, "You recognize him?"

"Nope. But ten gets you twenty he's our guy."

Chapter Twenty-Six

Blu stood against the wall of the back conference room at the Palmetto Pulse. The room was now empty except for some folding chairs where Patricia, Tess, and Crome sat around a matching temporary table. Josie set up trays of sandwiches and chips and had a cooler of drinks.

Everyone ate except for Crome and Tess.

Patricia said, "You better eat something."

"I'm on a liquid diet," Crome said, holding up his cup and vape pen.

"We ate while viewing the video feed," Tess said.

Blu said, "So what do we know?"

Tess, sitting next to Brack, said, "We know that Maureen and Harmony are missing. We know that Crome was contacted about Maureen's disappearance but none of us has been contacted about Harmony's. We think it has something to do with a past client of Blu Carraway Investigations. And we have a shadowy picture of a man who got on the mayor's boat thirty minutes before they did."

"There hasn't been a ransom request," Brack said.

Blu said, "It's been four days since Crome first got the picture and voicemail."

Tess asked, "You two aren't hiding anything, are you?"

"There's too much," Blu said.

"What do you mean, 'there's too much'?" Tess said.

"I mean there's too much to sort through," Blu said. "We've given you everything we can think of related to Maureen. We've only known you and Harmony for about a year."

"Then we have to get new information," Josie said.

Patricia's niece was one sharp young woman and he hoped she would be going to work for Blu Carraway Investigations when Patricia finally closed the doors to the Palmetto Pulse.

"That's why we're here," Crome huffed.

"What I mean," Josie said, "is you aren't going to find anything here. We need to retrace Maureen's and Harmony's steps."

"I already did Maureen's," Crome said.

"And we have Harmony's on video," Tess said. "She's right, though. How did the abductor know when and where to strike?"

She'd printed out pictures of the man. No one else had recognized him, either.

"He followed them."

Patricia said what everyone in the room was probably already thinking. "It could have easily been me instead of Harmony."

Blu said, "So he's an opportunist."

"Now there's a big word for ya," Crome said.

"Think about it," Blu said, "The guy's a planner, but he's flexible. If the mayor didn't know who he'd have on his boat until maybe an hour before he did, that didn't give our guy enough time to plan for who. He just planned for someone."

"But what if it hadn't been Harmony or Patricia?" Tess asked.

"Either he would have let sleeping dogs lie," Blu said, "sort of a 'no harm no foul' decision, or he would have taken someone else."

"Except they wouldn't have been related to us," Brack said.

"And we're back to that," Crome said.

"Unless—" Blu stopped himself. "Damn."

"Unless what?" Crome asked.

Blu looked at his partner. "Unless he was tracking Harmony."

*   *   *

Thursday afternoon

Crome listened to the logic coming from the team of people in the room. Those he'd been to war with, traded vodka shots with, played horseshoes with, and generally considered his friends. They were saying he and Blu were the targets of this and they were all saying it.

Two women were suffering only God knew what because of them. That's why he wasn't drinking right now. Booze slowed him down, took away from the caffeine and nicotine flowing in his veins.

"How the hell can someone keep two women chained up in this town with no one else knowing?" Tess asked.

Crome was about to dismiss it, but then caught himself. She was right, it would be hard.

Blu said, "They can't."

"What do you mean?" Patricia said. "Remember that wacko in Spartanburg that had that poor woman locked up in a warehouse for three months. It can be done."

"One, maybe," Crome said. "But two? It gets ex-po-nentially harder the more you add to the equation."

"He could be keeping them separated," Blu said.

Crome hadn't thought about that yet. That was why they made a good team. Together, they could cover all the angles.

Patricia said, "So he's got two different properties with a woman chained up in each? I don't see it."

"What if there are more than Maureen and Harmony?" Tess asked. "Or more than one abductor?"

Before Crome could think about what she'd said, Blu said, "I'll have Powers run down all the missing-persons cases. It's worth a shot. Maybe there's another one connected that we don't know about, yet." Blu stood, threw his plate and empty chip bag in the trash, and walked out.

Patricia's phone chirped. He watched her look at the display and drop her phone.

Chapter Twenty-Seven

Thursday six p.m.
DAY FOUR

Blu parked in front of the Pirate's Cove on the Isle of Palms and he and Crome walked up the stairs from the beach side and stood on the back deck. The message Patricia had received was that the mayor's body had washed up on the IOP beach. Tess had bolted out the door when she found out. Blu figured looking for a group of gawkers would be the easiest way to locate exactly which part of the beach.

The air temperature was a solid eighty-eight, the sky a clear blue. The surf was out from low tide, and most of the sand was covered with brightly colored beach towels and umbrellas.

The mayor, elected in 2007, had been popular with the citizens of the holy city. He'd helped bring in the cruise lines and the city had prospered through the recession. With all the industry in and around the city, he could have had a long tenure. He'd even hired Blu to do some personal security at one time.

Blu reminded himself to pull the client file on the mayor to see if anything was there, but he didn't think so. It made sense that the killer was tracking Patricia or Harmony. The mayor was collateral damage.

While Blu and Crome scanned the beach from their elevated perch, Brack's dog joined them, followed by Paige, the manager. She said, "You two are welcome to stay as long as you don't shoot up the place."

Blu got the impression she wasn't joking. "Fair enough."

Crome knelt to pet the dog. "You know who found the mayor?"

"Some tourists on a morning walk," she said. Paige looked down the beach at the crowd watching the police work from behind the tape line. "We really don't need this."

Charleston relied heavily on tourism. Vacationers didn't want to stumble across dead bodies. At least, not the tourists that they would want to have visiting and spending their hard-earned money on daiquiris and shrimp cocktails.

Crome didn't reply.

Shaking her head, Paige said, "I can't imagine what Maureen and Harmony are going through."

"Is Brack down there?" Blu asked, motioning toward the group of people.

"Yes," she said. "Is that where you're going next?"

Crome stood and started for the stairs. "Yep."

Paige said, "Can you take a couple trays of tea to the police officers?"

Blu and Crome each carried two drink trays of four teas. They found an area sectioned off by crime-scene tape that held back the crowd from members of the police force. Among the gawkers were Pelton and Tess.

"What're the police saying?" Blu asked.

"Nothing," Tess said, more than a hint of disappointment in her voice.

The IOP police chief, Ron Bates, saw the two new gawkers and came over. Six foot two and lean for being over fifty, he wiped sweat off his forehead, took one of the teas, and signaled for his men to do likewise.

Those that weren't gloved up and collecting evidence came over and grabbed teas of their own. The trays were empty in no time.

Crome asked, "What are you thinking?"

Bates sucked down half his tea and eyed him. "You must be

Mick Crome."

"Guilty," Crome said.

"Normally I wouldn't say anything, but I understand we have more to worry about than just the mayor."

The body had already been removed and it looked to Blu as if the police officers working the scene were combing through the sand.

"You find anything on him that might help us locate Harmony?" Tess asked.

"His pockets were empty, if that's what you mean," the chief said.

"Did he drown?" Blu asked.

"I don't know yet," the chief said. "He had a significant head wound."

Tess turned and walked away from the group. Pelton followed her.

Blu turned back to the chief. "Can you let me know when you have the time of death?"

The chief said, "You've had knowledge of a missing woman since Monday and I find out from Brack today. You have some nerve asking me for help now."

There was nothing Blu could say in reply. The chief was right. If Crome hadn't acted like a complete ass, maybe Blu would have considered bringing in the local authorities to help. He simply nodded.

After a moment, the chief looked away. "I'll make sure you know what I know. The mayor washed up on my beach, but I'm pretty sure he didn't die here. Charleston County will have to take this on. I'm not equipped to handle it, anyway."

"You guys find his boat?" Crome asked.

Still looking away, Bates said, "No."

* * *

Friday morning
DAY FIVE

Tess knew the mayor's body washing up changed everything, at least as far as Harmony's disappearance was concerned. Blu's friend, Detective Powers, was put in charge of the investigation. When Blu shared with him the video of Harmony and the mayor heading out on the boat along with the man who had boarded an hour before, he took notes and promised a delicate touch with the media. He also committed to having all the similar missing-persons cases reviewed.

The irony of the whole situation, at least as far as Tess was concerned, was that if the other media outlets got hold of the information, there was no telling how it would get spun. In a preliminary discussion, Powers mentioned a theory that Harmony could be working with the kidnapper.

She hadn't seen Blu get as upset as when he heard that. Crome had to separate his business partner from the detective. Objectively speaking, the theory could not be dismissed. What Blu was most likely trying to do was to keep Crome from blowing up. By taking the lead in the irrational reaction, he put Crome in the role of acting like an adult. It was a good play and it worked.

Otherwise, Crome might have pulled a gun and shot the detective.

What wasn't clear was any real linkage to Maureen and Harmony and the mayor. Therefore, Maureen was considered a separate case. It was assigned to a different detective in Myrtle Beach. Blu had tried to convince Powers that it would be double work for nothing and to keep them together, but no proof was there.

Tess knew this was a mistake for a lot of reasons. One of those reasons appeared when Crome elected himself to work with the Myrtle Beach detective and wanted to take off. The last thing she and Blu needed was Crome running on his own again. All the work done to rein him in would get blown out the window.

Chapter Twenty-Eight

Friday morning, the Pirate's Cove Bar
DAY FIVE

Amidst all the chaos, Crome watched as Brack Pelton made a call to Myrtle Beach. He put it on speaker.

It was answered on the second ring. "Brack?"

"What's up, Williams?"

"That's Detective Williams to you."

Smiling, Brack said, "That's why I'm calling. I've got you on speaker here in my bar."

"Yeah?"

Crome knew from a background check on Pelton that Detective Williams had helped track down the kid's uncle's killer a few years ago.

Brack said, "You guys caught a case, a missing person by the name of Maureen Lewis."

"It's not mine."

"How hard would it be for you to get it?"

It was a good idea and not entirely easy for Crome to admit as much.

"Now why would I want to add to my caseload?" Williams asked.

"Because then you could work with yours truly again."

"I remember something about getting fired in Charleston for doing exactly that."

"True," Brack said, "but you can't blame everything on me."

There was a pause in the conversation, as if Williams considered something.

"You there?" Brack asked.

"I'm here. I'm just trying to figure out what angle you're playing."

Brack looked at Crome. "I'm on my way to you along with a friend named Mick Crome."

"Mick Crome? He's a friend of yours?"

Crome was about to speak when Pelton held up a hand to cut him off.

"Yep."

The detective asked, "Is he there with you now? He's involved with this missing-person case?"

"It's his girlfriend."

"Oh no."

"Exactly."

"He's on his way here, too?"

"Yes."

"Well, I don't give a rip if he's listening or not. Can you control him?"

Pelton smiled. "I'm not going to say I'll be able to do that."

"You almost went to jail more than once," Williams said. "Riding with Mick Crome will turn that almost into a definite, you know."

"I get that impression."

"What about his partner, Carraway?"

"He's stuck here. The case has a few tentacles, one of which is in Myrtle Beach. The other is here and it includes the mayor."

"No kidding?" Williams asked. "And you believe they're linked? Anyone else think that? Any cops?"

"There's nothing you would be able to call evidence," Brack said.

"But you and Crome are heading this way?"

"Yes."

"How long?"

"We leave in ten minutes."

Crome said, "I'm going alone, Jarhead."

Brack covered the phone so Williams couldn't hear him say, "The hell you are."

Williams said, "Did you just throw that back at him? You know he's been known to kill people."

Uncovering the phone, Brack said, "I got this. We'll call you en route." He ended the call.

Crome stepped to Brack, his greater height caused Brack to have to look up. "Just what do you think you got here?"

"You," the kid said. "This situation."

"You're funny, you know that? If you hadn't found Hope that one time, I'd stuff you into that trash can over there."

"Put it back in your pants and let's get going."

Crome said, "I been around here longer than you, sonny. I got sources old enough to be your granddaddy."

"And they've been such a great help so far, let me tell you," Brack said.

Crome balled his fists. This kid did not back down for anything.

Blu stepped in. "We don't have time for this. Crome, ride with him. Either that or fight it out."

Crome chuckled. "Wouldn't be much of a fight."

"Yeah?" Blu said. "Personally I think he's crazier than you are. Plus he's only trying to help, which means you're the one acting like an idiot."

After a few more seconds of the stare down, Crome stepped away. "You really don't give a lick, do you, kid?"

"No one ever accused me of that before."

Crome headed for the door. "Come on. You can drive. I need a nap."

*   *   *

Friday morning

So much for a nap. Crome looked over at the speedometer, saw it crest ninety, and then took in Pelton's focus on the road, his hands at ten and two on the wheel, and thought this kid was crazier than he was.

"So who's this detective source of yours in Myrtle Beach?" Crome asked.

"He saved my life a few years ago. Doesn't concern himself too much with the gray area."

"No kidding?" Crome asked. He hadn't met too many cops who wouldn't collar him for suspicion of an illegal act, i.e. the gray area.

A squirrel ran out in front of the car. Crome barely had time to register it when the kid made a gentle correction with the steering.

Crome waited for the inevitable thump underneath but it didn't come. He looked back and saw the animal run off the road, down the berm, and into the woods. Most people would have jerked the wheel to try to avoid it, killed the animal anyway, and wiped out the car in one shot. The kid had a coolness about him. Blu had said he'd been a race car driver in a previous life.

To keep his mind off his lack of control at the moment, Crome asked, "So what do you like to shoot?"

Without taking his eyes off the road, Pelton said, "Forty-fives mostly. You?"

"Nine millimeter Glocks."

"Those are nice," the kid said, "but I like things a little more old school."

"Bikes and music, I agree with you," Crome said. "But firepower, I want the newest, baddest thing I can get my hands on."

"I heard you were more of a leg-breaker," Pelton said.

Crome chuckled. "Yeah, well that's only close up. I'd rather it not get that close, truth be told."

"Hmm."

They blew past the sign saying they'd just entered the Myrtle Beach city limits. Pelton let off the gas and let the compression from the five-liter engine of his Mustang slow them down. Crome preferred original Mustangs made before catalytic converters but this one was meaner than anything he could remember.

Pelton wheeled his car onto the main drag through South Myrtle and parked at a tourist trap bar and grill.

They got out of the car and walked inside.

Crome scanned the bar patrons and his eyes landed on the only one who could be the cop—a short, stalky guy with a receding hairline. The cop gave them a wave and Pelton led the way over to him.

The cop stood and shook the kid's hand. Then he turned his attention to Crome.

"Jim Wilson. I talked with Dorman. He sends his regards."

That caught Crome off guard. He'd heard the local cops hated Bert's Bar and had wanted to shut it down for some time now. To hear one acknowledge that he'd spoken with Bert Dorman, the owner, was something new. Maybe Pelton was right. Maybe this detective really didn't care about the gray areas. That's what Bert's Bar was, one big gray area.

He shook the detective's hand. "Mick Crome."

To Pelton, the detective said, "Did you really have to cruise ninety-five the whole way up here? You know how many favors I had to cash in just to keep my buddies from hauling you to jail?"

The kid smiled. "I knew you had me covered."

Wilson grunted.

Crome realized the kid really did have some pull. A license to speed was not something easily come by.

With a wave of his hand, Wilson invited them to sit at his table. "Thirsty?"

A waiter came over.

Pelton ordered an iced tea.

Crome got black coffee.

The waiter left and Wilson said, "Word is Maureen was taken

by someone not from here."

"How'd you come by that?" Pelton asked.

Wilson said, "I personally rolled all my sources. They're all saying the same thing. It's someone from out of town because they don't have a clue. These are people who know everything about everything. If a new cook sets up a meth lab, they know about it before the burner gets lit. They know when the fresh-off-the-bus sixteen-year-old turns her first trick. And they know within minutes which junkie just offed himself with a hot shot."

"What else do they know about this?" Crome asked.

Wilson smiled. "They know that if you find whoever kidnapped Maureen before the police do, you will kill them."

Crome thought about that.

"Look," Wilson said, leaning in, "some of them are people you know. You might not call them friends, but you know them. Even the ones who got their fingers broken by you are saying the same thing. None of them would show you any disrespect. They all fear you."

"You blowing smoke?" Pelton asked.

"Nope," Wilson said. "Your friend here has got quite a reputation in these parts. All over the damn state, really. No one who knows him would cross him for no reason. Some might do it for money, but it would take a hefty sum."

The waiter dropped off their drinks and left.

Crome took a swig of his coffee. It tasted burnt but at least it was hot. Not that iced crap Blu liked. He said, "So where should we be looking?"

Wilson replied, "I would have told you to talk to Skull, but your partner shot him down last year."

That made Crome chuckle. "That he did. So who's running things in the state, now?"

"With Skull out of the picture, the gangs have taken over. The Columbia Police have their hands full. Same with Charleston, although it's pretty much moved to the north side of town there."

"What about here?" Pelton asked.

Wilson sat back and looked at Crome. "If you want to know who's running things here, I suggest you have another talk with Dorman."

That was what they drove all the way up here for?

Crome said, "That's all you've got?"

"No," Wilson said. "I have something else."

"What's that?" Pelton asked.

"We found Maureen's car. I figured you might want to look it over."

Chapter Twenty-Nine

Friday mid-morning

Crome had a notion to strangle the detective. What kind of person played a game like that in the middle of a hostage situation? And that's exactly what they were in. Maureen and Harmony and the murdered mayor. What the hell?

And before Crome could rip the man's head off, Pelton leaned in almost face to face with his supposed detective friend. "This isn't particularly funny, Wilson."

The detective gave a smirk. "No, it isn't. And I'm not trying to play a game here."

Crome said, "It sure sounds like you are to me."

"Yeah?" The detective looked at Crome. "Well, I'm sorry about that. But what I'm about to give you could get me fired."

The kid didn't respond. Neither did Crome.

Wilson stood. "Follow me." They followed him outside to his unmarked Charger. "Get in."

Pelton gave Crome the front seat and didn't crack any jokes about age before beauty or anything like that. In fact, no one said anything as Wilson drove them down the main tourist drag of Myrtle Beach, moving with the summer traffic.

Nothing about it made sense to Crome. They should be working around the cops, not with them. They should be hauling ass in any direction that gets them closer to finding the women. Logic would say never in a million years should they be riding in a cop car to the police impound.

Except Wilson didn't take them to the impound or even the police station. After less than ten minutes crawling along in traffic, he pulled into a Public Parking lot, pressed the button at the entrance, received a ticket, waited until the gate raised, and then drove in.

Pelton said, "What the—?"

Crome spotted Maureen's ten-year-old Honda ahead. Next to it was a spot blocked off by orange cones.

Wilson pulled up to the open spot and put the car in park. He got out and moved the cones. Crome got out, opened the back door for Pelton, and both of them walked over to Maureen's car.

The detective said, "Hold up."

They stopped.

He said, "Let me give you some latex gloves. The car hasn't been processed yet. And before you ask, there are no cameras covering the lot."

It finally sunk in what was going on. The detective was giving them first crack at the car. However he'd been able to swing it, Wilson was acting as if he were one of them and not like an officer of the law. Whatever Crome thought about the man, it all vanished. This guy was as unorthodox as they came.

They watched Wilson park his car in the saved spot. He got out and opened the trunk.

Crome took an offered pair of gloves from Wilson, slipped them on, and walked over to Maureen's car.

The summer sun was hot and the surrounding buildings blocked them from feeling the ocean breeze.

"Detective?" Crome asked. "You got a couple screwdrivers?"

"You know how to get in?" the detective asked.

"I do," Crome said.

The detective gave him a smile as if saying, "Of course you'd know."

Crome didn't care. In fact, he wouldn't care if the detective insulted his dearly departed mother at this point. The gift he was giving them trumped anything else at the moment.

Taking the offered tools, Crome pried the window open, slid his hand in, and opened the door.

The alarm started honking. The car was a decade old, but even ten-year-old Hondas had theft-deterrent systems.

Crome bent down in the driver's footwell and yanked out a couple wires, silencing the shriek.

"I'm impressed," the detective said. "You missed your calling."

Crome grinned. "Blu and I used to work repo back when we started out." It was those jobs that kept them in business when nothing else was walking through the door.

Wilson said, "Hell, Brack. Between your wife and your friend here, nothing is secure."

Blu had told Crome that Pelton's wife was an expert at picking locks and had taught the kid, who apparently was a fast study. The problem was everything today was electronic. Breaching the mechanical systems was the easy part. It was the circuitry that was the real challenge. Crome had bypassed the lock and silenced the alarm, but they wouldn't be able to start Maureen's car. It was quite dead.

Before he did anything else, Crome gave the car a thorough look.

Pelton and Wilson held back, letting him take it in.

Nothing appeared out of place at first glance. Maureen took care of the things she owned and her car was no exception. It was old and worn but the interior was clean and vacuumed and she did not let trash accumulate.

So, when his hand stumbled across a bag underneath the driver's seat, he knew it shouldn't have been there and on any normal day wouldn't have been.

It was a bag from a big-chain drug store. He pulled it out and examined it. Inside were a receipt and an empty box of pills women took for cramps.

Wilson said, "What have you got?"

Crome held up the bag. "There's one of these places not too far from Maureen's trailer. She doesn't leave trash in her car. I'd say this was from the last time she drove it."

"We should check their cameras," Pelton said. "See if they tell us anything. Is the receipt in the bag? It'll give us a time stamp."

Friday, mid-morning

Blu had a lot on his mind. Crome was barely holding it together. Maureen was still missing and it had been five days. Harmony got caught up in something and had also disappeared. The mayor washing up on IOP Beach may or may not be connected to Maureen's disappearance. And Billie had not given him an answer on his proposal, nor even returned his calls and texts in over a month.

Overall, most things were not going well. He worried about the missing women. He worried about his friend. He worried about Brack Pelton getting involved. He worried about Brack's wife. He worried about Tess. And Patricia. And Billie. And he worried about his daughter. That was a lot for one man to handle at one time.

Tess sat with him at the rooftop bar of the Pirate's Cove, both of them facing the ocean. Tourists covered the beach below with a layer of brightly colored towels, folding chairs, and large umbrellas. The atmosphere was one of American optimism, but Blu didn't feel any of it at the moment.

Shelby snored softly at Tess' feet.

A line of five pelicans glided overhead, momentarily distracting Blu. It had made him happy when a colony of the magnificent birds nested in the marsh by his home last summer. He spent many mornings waiting for the eggs to turn into hatchlings.

Paige brought him back to reality when from behind the bar, she asked, "You heard from Brack?"

"No," Blu said.

Apparently Blu didn't have a monopoly on worrying. Paige,

youthful and beautiful, had begun to show a few lines of concern on her forehead. Blu had the impression that being around Brack Pelton would do that to anyone. Being in business with him might even be worse.

But, then again, Blu had Mick Crome. When he didn't disappear for three years on a drunken, violent escapade, Crome defied his friend, tried to go his own way, and only failed at his attempt to alienate those around him.

Paige stood facing them, her arms folded across her chest. As almost an afterthought, Blu had the impression she wanted more than a one-word answer. He didn't have it.

"They're bound to call sooner or later," Tess offered.

It didn't sound convincing to Blu.

Blu took a hit on his vaporizer. Until Maureen had gone missing, he'd been weaning himself off of the device. His goal had been to be smoke and vapor free by the end of the year, but it didn't look like he was going to make it.

Tess took a sip of her virgin Bloody Mary.

Paige looked around at all the bottles surrounding her. "I need a drink."

Blu's phone buzzed. He looked at the screen, didn't recognize the number, and answered.

A familiar female voice said, "Blu?"

It was Harmony.

Chapter Thirty

Crome stayed back and watched Detective Wilson badge his way to access the video from the drug store. Normally a warrant was required, but the store manager, a thin woman about Crome's age who smelled of cigarettes and spoke with a husky voice, seemed to take a liking to Pelton. The kid, to his credit, played it up nicely, thanking the lady profusely and hinting about maybe having to return to view other videos.

The men crowded around the woman in a small office in the back of the store and watched the computer screen as she loaded the footage from the night on the receipt. They were interested in viewing the cameras inside the store and the parking lot.

The first video covered the register area. After catching a few glimpses of Maureen walking around the store, it showed her make her purchase with a twenty-dollar-bill and then walk out. At this angle, there didn't appear to be anyone suspicious following her.

Pelton said, "Wait a minute."

Crome caught what the kid had seen as well. There was a man in the store who followed Maureen out.

Wilson asked the woman, whose name was Marge, if she could load the footage from the other cameras.

She gave a nod, glanced at Brack with big eyes, and said, "Anything to help our local police force. I tell ya, you guys have a tough job."

Pelton put a hand on her shoulder. "Thanks, Marge. You don't know how much we appreciate what you're doing."

It might be a stretch to call it impersonating an officer, but

Crome got the impression Marge thought they were all on the job. And none of them seemed to want to clarify anything.

She loaded another video, this one taken from a different angle in the store. It showed Maureen walk down an aisle, stop, and remove something from the shelf. It also showed a man tracking her from the aisle behind the one she was in. In the video, Crome couldn't tell if he was the same man from the marina video. He also couldn't tell if Maureen sensed the man behind her or not. Normal people were typically not suspicious of those around them. Maureen could have just assumed it was another shopper in the store and dismissed him.

After she made her selection, Crome watched the man track Maureen to the counter, hanging back. He said, "That's got to be the bastard."

Marge said, "You're saying the man did something to the woman?"

"Not in the store," Wilson said. "But we suspect that he might have accosted her outside. Can we see the footage of the parking lot?"

"Um," Marge began.

"No one here's in trouble," Wilson said, reassuringly. "The woman's missing and we're trying to figure out who took her."

"That's terrible," Marge said, a hand to her mouth. She returned her hand to the mouse and loaded another view.

The three of them watched Maureen exit the store, opening the bag as she walked. Her focus was on the package and she didn't notice the man following ten feet behind. This view was better and in it Crome recognized the man as the same one from the marina video. In this scene, the man caught up with Maureen as she slipped a bottle of pills in her purse and opened her car door. He popped her in the face. If it hadn't been his girlfriend, Crome might have been somewhat impressed with the speed with which the assailant moved.

Marge said, "Oh my God."

As Maureen fell, the man caught her in his arms, picked her up and loaded her in the car, over the center console and onto the passenger seat. It took less than ten seconds.

The man picked up a set of keys that she dropped, got in the driver's seat, and drove away. No one else saw what had happened except the camera. Crome thought the kidnapper was betting on no one viewing the footage of his assault.

"That poor woman," Marge said.

Wilson said, "Thank you so much for your cooperation. We may need copies of that if you can get them for us."

Crome walked out of the office, through the store, and out the exit. Outside, he pulled out his vaporizer and took a few hits. He'd kept his mind as blank as he could while watching what happened to Maureen and now thoughts of vengeance flooded in.

Who in the hell was this guy?

The automatic door opened and Pelton exited. He came over to Crome. "You know the guy?"

"No, but at least now we know Maureen and Harmony are linked."

"Something like that happened to Darcy a few years ago," Pelton said. "I shot the man who took her four times."

"He die?" Crome asked.

"He's doing life upstate. It was Patricia's thirty-two and I hit him in the chest."

"Shoulda aimed for the head," Crome said.

"You're telling me." The kid looked away, not miffed. More like he was thinking. "At least we have a picture of him."

"Maureen didn't have a chance." And it really burned Crome up inside.

"She's a good person," Pelton said. "From what I hear, she's also a strong woman. We'll find her."

At the moment, it was exactly what Crome needed to hear, although he wouldn't admit it.

Wilson came out, held up a jump drive, and said, "Marge hooked us up. Let's roll."

Friday, noon

To Harmony, Blu said, "Can you talk?"

Meaning, did someone have a gun to her head.

Harmony said, "Um, I wanted to let you know that I'm okay."

"Is Maureen with you?"

There was a hesitation in her voice when she said, "I've got a good view of things."

That didn't make sense, but Blu guessed it was code and he'd figure it out later. "What did you call to tell me?"

"I-I have a message for you," she said.

"Yes?" He pointed to a pen and paper and Paige quickly handed them to him.

"There's more coming."

"Yes?" Blu asked, not understanding.

"That's all."

He needed to keep her talking. "We all miss you."

As if in a hurry, she rattled off, "I miss shots by PC's sister."

Again, he'd figure out what that meant later. "When are you coming home?"

Her voice broke. "I don't—"

The call ended.

Friday, noon

In the Charger, Crome stayed quiet.

Pelton asked Wilson, "So how'd you find the car?"

"When you called, I put out an APB. One of our units came across it. The lots don't ever empty completely so it didn't really stand out."

"Damn," Crome said.

"What?" Wilson asked.

"We forgot to check out the video from the other parking lot cameras," he said. "We might have the guy's plate number."

Wilson said, "I got it all. Let's go to my office."

Pelton pulled out his phone and answered a call.

Crome halfway listened until the kid said, "What?"

Then he focused in and heard him say, "You heard from Harmony? What about Maureen?"

There was a pause as Pelton listened.

Then he said, "We've got video of Maureen's abduction. We're on our way back to the Myrtle Beach PD to see if we can get a license plate number off his car."

The call ended. Blu had put it on speaker so Tess and Paige could hear what Pelton had to say.

Paige said, "Thank God Brack and Crome are okay."

It hadn't occurred to Blu to worry about their well being. He looked at what he'd written down from his conversation with Harmony.

She's okay.

She said she's got a good view of things.

There's more coming.

She misses shots by PC's sister.

She doesn't – call ended.

He said, "I think she's telling us she's with Maureen."

"But who is PC's sister?"

"I don't know," Blu said, "but I'm thinking she went off script because he cut her off after that."

Tess sank in her chair.

Blu asked, "You don't know anyone with the initials PC who has a sister?"

She did a slow shake of her head as if still racking her brain to solve the puzzle.

"Maybe it isn't a person," Blu said.

"PC?" Tess asked. "PC...Yes!"

Blu caught on.

In unison they said, "Pirate's Cove."

Blu said, "The other bar on Kiawah. What's it called?"

Paige said, "Reggie's Shipwreck."

"We've got to go there," Blu said. "And I've got to call Pelton."

Tess dug out her phone. "I'm on it."

Unlike the Pirate's Cove, Brack's second bar was not ocean front. It was a two-story, all-wood pub across the street from the beach. Blu walked in with Tess and felt as if nothing was wrong and they were missing something.

Because Kiawah was upscale, Paige and Brack had transformed what used to be a vacant family restaurant into a very nice place. It had a big, mahogany bar in the middle of the place like in the TV show *Cheers*. The floor was hardwood and the walls were white and trimmed in wood. The ceiling was high and had exposed rafters and braces. And from what Pelton had said, the souvenir shop made almost as much money as liquor sales.

The clientele was older and richer than at the other bar and everyone seemed to be couples.

It took a few moments, and then Blu was ready to leave.

Tess said, "She didn't mention inside the bar. Maybe there's something outside?"

"Shots by PC's sister," Blu said.

They stepped outside and looked around. Across the street were two ocean front bars. And to the right of them was—

Blu took off running.

Tess screamed at him but he didn't stop.

He took the steps down to the dock of the Kiawah Marina two at a time and felt more than heard Tess on his heels.

Slowing to a stop, he put a hand out to stop Tess from continuing.

"You don't think?" Tess asked.

"It's got to be where the mayor's boat is. But we need the police on this."

He called Powers.

Blu and Tess watched as the Kiawah Police department roped off the area around the mayor's boat. They were also getting a warrant to view any of the footage of the security cameras in the vicinity.

Powers called Blu.

He said, "Good work on finding the boat."

"It was Harmony." Blu said. "They find anything? No one's talking to us here."

"I know," Powers said. "That's why I'm calling."

"Well?"

"As far as they can tell, the boat got wiped down, i.e. no prints."

Blu said, "Figures."

"After that," Powers said, "they tore the boat apart looking for anything. All they found was that someone had written "MLM ECO" in red lipstick on the bottom of one of the cushions. Does that mean anything to you?"

Blu couldn't think of anything. He asked Tess, who shook her head.

Powers said, "They'll keep looking. You guys should come back to Charleston. If the police there find anything, they'll call me. Also, I need the number. We'll see if we can track the call."

Blu gave him his number and the number Harmony called in on. He also told Powers where he was when he received the call. Powers thanked him and hung up.

Chapter Thirty-One

Friday, early afternoon

Crome watched from an empty chair in the next cubicle as Wilson ran the plate in the police database. It came back to a stolen car, the same make and model as the Toyota Camry the man had gotten out of at the drug store. And the car was still missing.

It also didn't help that the picture sent to Crome was from the hotel in Charleston, meaning the man had transported Maureen from Myrtle Beach.

Crome leaned against Pelton's Mustang outside of the Myrtle Beach Police Headquarters deep in thought. The man must have already reserved the room in Charleston before he abducted Maureen. That required some serious planning as did stealing the car.

The Camry had a Myrtle Beach address. Wilson wanted to check it out next but Crome could tell he didn't want their help.

Pelton, either not sensing the same thing or not caring, tried to strong arm Wilson into letting them go with him but he didn't budge. Crome had to step between them and that surprised him. Normally he'd have been the hothead getting in the cop's face. But Pelton needed to be refereed. He stood nearby, fuming.

Crome respected the kid even more after that.

"You believe that crap?" Pelton asked.

"Yep."

Pelton leaned against his car next to Crome and sighed.

"Don't take it personal, Brack," Crome said. "He's just doing his job."

"He's got the hottest case in town now thanks to us and he cuts us out."

Crome said, "Didn't you tell me the last time you two went out on a mission together he lost his job?"

He couldn't tell for sure, but Crome thought Pelton might have let his chin drop a bit but then recovered.

"You know what we need to ask Wilson, don't you?" Crome said.

Pelton pushed away from the car. "No."

"Where was the car stolen from and when?"

"Because," Pelton said, finishing Crome's thought for him, "if it's a business, we can check the security cameras there, too."

"Yep."

Reaching into his pocket and retrieving his phone, Pelton said, "Hot damn."

The lot to the large retail store where the Camry was stolen was not too far from the drug store where Maureen was snatched. Wilson said the owner had left the car, and its AC, running with their dog in it and came out to find the Camry and Fido gone.

The dog, a Yorkie, wouldn't have put up much of a fight as the owner had said it was friendly. Fortunately for everyone involved, animal control picked up the chipped pooch and, after a gladly paid fine, returned him to his owners.

This time, there was no friendly Marge to shortcut the legal system and allow them carte blanche access to the security camera footage. The manager of the retail store, a pleasant man named George, explained that he would honor any court order request.

That didn't help them. But sharing space next door to the big box store in the shopping center strip mall was a locally-owned Chinese restaurant. The owners also had security cameras including one with an exceptional view of the parking lot.

And they were big fans of the police department. Apparently an off-duty officer stopped vandals from defacing their storefront the previous year and the owners were forever grateful.

They had a teenage son who worked the computer system for Crome, Wilson, and Pelton. The video, grainier than the system Marge worked with, panned a good portion of the lot.

Crome pointed at the screen. "Is that our Camry?"

"By golly you're right," Wilson said. To the teenager, he said, "Can you go back to when the car first parks?"

The restaurant owner's son, David, moved the mouse and made a few clicks. He timed it just right and hit play seconds before the car pulled in and parked.

A woman, David's mother, brought in a tray of egg rolls for them. Pelton offered to pay but she vehemently refused, saying they were honored to help.

Crome munched on an egg roll covered in hot mustard and watched the driver of the car park, get out, lock the door with a key, and walk into the store. They had told the police they left the car running, so they must have had a second set of keys.

The dog could be seen peeking through the window.

Five minutes passed and then someone else—the man they'd observed kidnapping Maureen—approached the car, looked around, popped the lock, let the dog out, and drove off.

Crome watched the dog, now obviously confused, wander around the lot, narrowly avoiding getting run over more than once. It was a miracle the pooch made it out alive.

Pelton said, "At least the dog survived."

"No kidding," Wilson said.

After another five minutes, the dog no longer in the picture, the car owner returned to find his car gone. They watched him look around panic stricken, take out his phone, and make a call.

Crome had a hunch the car owner wasn't involved and now he was convinced of it. No real dog lover would do what was done to the Yorkie, letting it roam free in a busy parking lot.

Wilson asked, "Did you guys see where the man showed up

from?"

They didn't, and had David rerun the footage several times before giving up. The man had come from the side and they could not determine how he got there or from which car.

Wilson asked David, "Are you friends with any of the other business owners here?"

"We know a few of them," David said. "You want me to see if they have any cameras set up?"

It was a good thought. Maybe they could trace the man back to his car from another section of the lot. He couldn't be that far away since he'd have to know the Camry's engine was running. He'd have to be close enough to hear it.

Two doors down was an electronics store. David, with his glasses and teenage acne, was a regular shopper there. It was this relationship, above all the others, that gave Crome, and by extension Blu, the break they needed. The abductor had parked directly in front of this store. The camera system, given that the store sold electronics, was better than Marge's. The video was crystal clear, and viewed on the thirty-two-inch flatscreen in the manager's office, gave them a perfect shot of the license plate.

Wilson said, "Gotcha."

Crome could taste the blood of his enemy.

Chapter Thirty-Two

Friday afternoon

Blu put his phone on speaker while Pelton rattled off what they'd found. Of course Crome wouldn't make the call. He was probably too busy contemplating the many different ways he was going to disembowel the individual who started this whole mess. At least Pelton and Crome were back in the Mustang and on their way home.

The detective that Pelton and Crome had worked with had been very helpful. Following his new protocol of working with the police, Blu shared his information first with Powers. Pelton had emailed a name and plate number.

In the long stretch in the middle of the Francis Marion National Forest, Crome awoke from a nap and found Pelton cruising at a hundred and ten miles an hour, the car's V-8 burbling along.

The kid had a lead foot.

Crome asked, "Can you get a move on?"

"Might not be able to stop if a deer runs out as it is."

Either Pelton didn't realize Crome had been kidding or was ignoring it. Crome liked him anyway. He liked it even more that his source had paid off big. Blu was tracking the abductor down as they spoke. Patricia had some pull with the mayor's deputy and they were busy getting the paper trail in order for when the guy was brought down.

Friday afternoon

Blu had a name that didn't set off any alarms and an address that didn't mean anything to him either. And he had the initials MLM ECO. At least he had something.

He also had Tess. More like he was stuck riding shotgun in her car.

"You're sure you don't recognize the name?" she asked.

"No." He pulled a nine millimeter Glock from his waistband and verified the chambered round for the fifth time. The act was done more out of habit than necessity. A round was always chambered. It settled his nerves. So did vaping and he did that next.

"What flavor is that?"

"Blackberry."

"It's different than what you normally have."

She was right. He normally liked one of the tobacco flavors.

"You pay attention to my vape choices?" he asked.

She turned and gave him her made-for-TV grin. With her dark-rimmed glasses, the smirk really got to him. But he had to stop himself from doing something stupid. He had Billie, or at least he hoped he still had Billie. He would know for sure if she ever called him back.

Tess said, "I know a lot about you. And Crome."

"Like what?"

"You worry a lot. About your daughter. About Billie. About getting too close to me and Harmony."

"Yeah?" What concerned him most was how close to target she'd hit.

"Yes. And you worry about Crome."

"Wouldn't you?" he asked.

"He's a grown man. I think he can take care of himself."

"He didn't do a good job of that for a long time," he said. "And not lately, either."

"You're wondering if Billie is going to say yes. And you're wondering what you're going to do if she doesn't."

"That's enough," he said. She was cutting deep.

"You asked," she said.

"What about you?"

"What about me?"

He leaned forward and stuck the gun in his back waistband. "You and Harmony hit this town like a wrecking ball in the wake of Darcy Pelton's absence. You both get a lot handed to you because of how you look."

"How do we look?"

"You know what I mean." He felt his cheeks flush. "People underestimate you in particular. Harmony wears her visage on her sleeve. You keep people a few arms' lengths away. It makes you more dangerous than she is."

"Dangerous?" she asked. "You think I'm dangerous, too?"

"In a way," he said. "Crome's also dangerous, but in a different way. He will kill for the right reason. You, on the other hand, can gut a man without him even knowing it."

"Do you think I would do that to you?" she asked.

"No," he said and meant it. "I wouldn't let you."

The smirk was back.

This conversation would not—should not—have occurred with someone still in their twenties.

They pulled to a stop at a light. She leaned over and kissed him on the lips.

He didn't stop her.

It felt more intimate than he expected, not that he even expected be kissed. Especially by her. There was passion and longing and understanding.

Straightening up in time to see the light turn green, she accelerated.

He vowed to himself that no one would ever know about what just happened.

Luckily, his cell phone buzzed in his pocket and he was able to change his thought pattern. It was Powers.

"Yo," Blu answered, still flustered from Tess' act of what he really hoped was pity.

"I'm standing here at that address you gave me with three other units."

"You find the women?" he asked.

"There's no one here."

"Damn." Blu didn't know what to do next, so he said, "Thanks" and ended the call.

Friday afternoon

Crome wanted to punch something, but didn't think Pelton would appreciate him hammering on the interior of his car. Especially after he said it had been a gift from his wife. So, he sat there seething.

The lead had just fallen apart.

The address the police had gotten from the license plate was to a house the police verified had a layer of dust covering the empty interior. The women were gone, probably dead, and the guy was in the wind. He'd vanished, never to return unless he decided to pick off another one of their friends and make them disappear as well.

As if reading his mind, Pelton said, "This sucks."

"No kidding."

They were on the Cooper River Bridge on their way to meet Blu, Tess, and Detective Powers and the three units he'd brought with him at the empty house. The only intel they'd been able to get that was worthwhile, or so he thought.

Crome pulled his phone out, made a call, and was surprised when it was answered.

"Yes?"

The bastard who really needed to die in the most horrific manner Crome could come up with actually answered the phone.

"I'm coming for you," Crome said, "and God won't be able to help you."

The man laughed. "I wouldn't expect anything less, Mick. But first you have to find me. How's that working out for you?"

The call ended.

Pelton said, "You've got his number?"

Crome ignored him and made another call.

After the call from Crome, Blu explained to Powers what they needed, and added, "And I mean right now."

Powers listened, nodded, and made a call.

If they could triangulate the signal from the man's phone, they might have a shot.

Why the hell the guy actually had the phone on and answered it was a tactical mistake. Either that, or he already had it covered in some way.

It was all they had left. It was a long shot, and if it didn't work, they were back to square one and none of them wanted to be back to square one.

Powers ended his call. "They're on it. I had to use my last favor. But we'll have something."

Tess said, "The guy actually answered his phone?"

"Yes," Blu said, "and I hope it's the last mistake of his life."

Chapter Thirty-Three

Rooftop bar, downtown Charleston, Friday, five p.m.

Crome hated waiting. It meant someone else was in control. Pinpointing cell phone signals was something neither he, nor Blu, nor Tess, nor Patricia, nor Pelton, nor even Darcy could do. It required pull with the feds who did it for the local police. And sometimes they weren't quick about it. The last thing Crome wanted to be doing was waiting on the government. After all, he'd done his darnedest to fly under the radar and avoid the government as much as possible. The only reason he filed tax returns was because it was a federal crime not to. Otherwise, he'd be completely off the grid.

The group sat at a large table at the Terrace bar overlooking Marion Square.

Blu said, "Shut the hell up."

Everyone including Crome looked at him. Crome was quite sure he hadn't said anything.

"That's right," Blu said. "Your thoughts are screaming at me."

"You shut the hell up," Crome said. It was a game they played to pass the time. And it annoyed everyone around them, which was the objective.

"Are you guys for real?" Pelton asked.

"Don't start something you can't finish, kid," Crome said.

Egging on Pelton was even more fun. He didn't back down.

And he didn't this time either, "You talk real tough for

someone your age."

"Yeah," Crome said. "Well, this old man is about to kick your ass."

Pelton smiled. "Really? I'm sure you think that. Up until your partner has to save you from the beating of your life."

The kid probably got beat up more times than he really should have only because he couldn't keep his mouth shut.

"He's got you there," Blu chuckled.

Tess said, "Do you boys always overcompensate?"

The men were saved from any further humiliation by a call to Blu's phone. It was Powers. Blu hit the speaker.

"Carraway?" Powers asked.

"Yes."

"Got some news."

Crome felt himself inch to the edge of his chair, ready to jump up and run.

"Yes?" Blu replied.

"The feds tracked the call to Folly Beach."

Everyone at the table stood up.

Blu asked, "You got a location?"

"As a matter of a fact I do."

It was a stone's throw from Crome's place.

Blu looked at Crome who was already on his way to the exit.

Patricia took out a hundred-dollar-bill, handed it to the waitress, and told her to keep the change. The tab for the one round for the six of them was probably around eighty dollars.

They all took the stairs down.

Crome followed Pelton who pressed the unlock button on his key fob and got into his car. Blu watched Crome barely have time to get himself in and close his door before Pelton laid two black tire marks on Calhoun Street.

Darcy said, "They deserve each other."

Blu jumped into the driver's seat of Tess' convertible. "Get in."

To his surprise, she obeyed. The car had keyless ignition and he pressed the start button. They left Darcy and Patricia to themselves as they accelerated away.

Calhoun Street was the last point that King Street went in both directions. Blu took a right heading away from the direction of the Battery and followed Pelton. Or tried to follow Pelton, as he slid his car around the corner and hammered it toward Seventeen which would take them to Folly Beach.

Friday, five p.m.

The man laughed to himself. If Mick Crome was able to trace the signal, he was sure the biker wannabe lost his lunch when he heard the location. It wasn't that he was inside the biker's house, but sitting in front of it, under an umbrella amongst all the other folks on the beach in front of it.

He'd been waiting for this, praying for it actually. In fact, he'd spent several hours each day over the last week in this very spot just in case Crome got the idea to call.

It was perfect. And now he could head home.

As soon as the call had ended, he'd pulled the sim card, packed up his stuff, walked back to his SUV, ditching the phone along the way, and went home.

To the women.

Who were waiting for him.

God, he loved that. They were like pets, relying on him for everything from basic sustenance to affirmation.

They were his to do with as he pleased. And no one would take that from him. Not now.

It made up for so much. Like when his woman got taken away from him. Why had he waited so long to get his revenge? He'd been distracted by his other causes. But when he saw Blu Carraway being interviewed in front of that burned out bait shop last year, he found a new cause. One that was for his benefit alone. He'd been so focused on saving the planet he'd forgotten about his own needs. Not any more. He would get his revenge, and he didn't care if the world knew why or not. This was for him.

At the moment, Crome appreciated the kid's driving skills. Pelton threaded the muscle car in and out of traffic faster than an industrial sewing machine through a bolt of cloth.

And he wasn't slowing down.

The car was wicked fast and the roar of the pipes was almost as good as his Harley's.

"What's the plan?" the kid asked as he drove.

"You get me there first and I'll take care of everything. You can keep your hands clean."

"That's not what I asked, Crome."

"That's the answer you're getting."

"What if I pull over and let Blu get there first?" he asked.

Crome almost took out his gun and shot him except it wouldn't do either of them any good as long as the car was in motion when he did it.

He said, "Don't make threats like that."

Downshifting, Pelton mashed the gas pedal and they rocketed around a garbage truck "Then don't shine me on."

Pelton really did have a violence addiction. It was going to get him killed one of these days, Crome was almost sure of it. And then Darcy would be a widow and Paige would get his bars.

Blu was not happy. Pelton was just too good of a driver and his car was much faster than Tess'. That meant they'd get to the house first. Except that he had the feeling the guy with a death wish who abducted Maureen and Harmony and killed the mayor wouldn't be where the Federal Bureau of Investigations said he was.

He handed his phone to Tess. "Call Powers back and see if the signal moved."

So far she hadn't complained about how hard he drove her "cute" little car. It had scoot, but not a V-8 like Pelton's Mustang, which they could no longer see ahead of them.

From his periphery, Blu saw Tess tap the screen a few times and then put the phone up to her ear.

She said, "This is Tess Ray. Blu wants to know if the signal moved." There was a pause as she listened to his response. Then she said, "Thanks." She lowered the phone and said. "You can pull over."

Chapter Thirty-Four

Pelton was faster and beat Crome out of the car, his forty-five drawn. If his own adrenaline weren't pegged, Crome would contemplate who wanted to kill someone more, him or Pelton.

The front door was still locked, just like Crome left it. With Pelton standing on the left side of the door, Crome inserted his key, turned the knob, and pushed the door in.

They waited for the inevitable resulting gunfire, their backs to the walls beside the doorway. It didn't come.

Pelton swung his forty-five into the open door and entered.

Crome followed, his Glock drawn.

There was nothing.

Everything was the way he remembered leaving it.

They cleared the home room by room.

They found nothing.

Pelton clicked the safety on and stuck the forty-five down his back waistband.

Crome felt his phone buzz, looked at the screen, saw BLU, and answered.

"Nobody here besides me and Billy the kid," Crome said.

Tess said, "The FBI told Powers the signal vanished right after you called and hasn't returned."

He didn't reply.

"There's something else," she said.

"Well spill it," Crome said after she didn't continue.

"The feds told Powers that phone has been pinging the signal in front of your house five hours a day for the last seven days."

"You're telling me the guy's been camped out in my backyard for the past week?" Crome asked, gripping the phone tighter with each word.

"No," she said, her voice measured. "I'm telling you what Powers told me."

"Same difference." He ended the call.

Pelton said, "I'm still hung up on the camera thing from Myrtle Beach."

"Yeah? Well good for you." All he was thinking was how pissed off he was that they chased another rabbit down a hole that had too many directions to follow.

"How well do you know your neighbors?"

Crome had to slow his thoughts down to a manageable level in order to think about what Pelton was asking. He looked at the kid.

Pelton smiled. "See what I'm asking."

"No."

"My bars," Pelton continued, "have more cameras than your bank. Some are obvious because we advertise them with "Smile for the camera" signs. Others, well, not so much. The only places we don't have coverage are the bathrooms. Everywhere else is under twenty-four-hour surveillance."

"Blu told me it helped you guys get the Hollander brothers."

A year ago, the same time Blu's daughter was kidnapped, the whole thing kicked off with a shootout in Pelton's bar. And it ended very badly for several men, including the two who started the gunplay. Crome had watched the footage of Pelton shooting it out with two professional killers.

Regarding Pelton's question, Crome did not know his neighbors. Most of them were vacation renters and rotated in and out all summer long. He said, "I don't know them, but who we need to be looking for are the home owners who live here year-round. Most of them don't."

Pelton pulled out his phone and made a call.

When it was answered, he said, "Hey, Honey."

Crome almost chuckled. The kid was calling his wife, the same woman he'd just left high and dry at the rooftop bar when they sped off. Now he'd see how well he could smooth things out.

After a pause, Pelton said, "I know. I'm sorry about that."

Another pause.

"Me, too. What we need is information about the owners of the homes surrounding Crome's. Can you or Patricia find out if any live there year-round?"

If anyone in the county could, it was those two.

"Thanks, Honey." He ended the call.

Crome eyeballed his friend. "She forgave you that fast? She's a keeper."

"My wife can handle anything except another woman. As long as I come home to her, I'm good."

"Easy enough." He chuckled. "Your wife is impressive. Of course, my problem is I've seen the talent in your bars. I'd have to sell both of them to even stand a chance of keeping her."

They got in the car and Pelton fired up the five-liter motor. "Yeah, well I've already been around the block. My first wife was amazing. I've struck gold twice now with Darcy and haven't met anyone else worth screwing it all up for."

"And may you never, kid. May you never."

Crome could have been jealous of what Pelton had, except he could never live that kind of life. He loved his Harley, but like everything else in his life, it was just a means to an end.

Pelton killed the engine and said, "I got another idea."

Friday early evening

Blu listened to Pelton's idea, liked it, and hoped it would pan out. Since Powers was so helpful the last time Tess called, he had her call him again. The request was simple, and probably already done.

Check the history of the phone and see if the guy ever got sloppy. It was a long shot, but that's all they had. In fact, long shots were all they'd been going on since Maureen first got taken.

Tess did her thing and Powers, like every other man on the Charleston Peninsula and surrounding counties who'd ever come in contact with her or her professional sister, agreed to give her more than she'd asked for. The "more" coming in the form of having patrol units at the ready in case more locations were found. It was also a long shot.

She hung up.

Blu said, "Maybe there is a place for you at Blu Carraway Investigations."

Tess handed the phone back.

He felt the urge to kiss her and tried to fight it. But it was all for naught. She leaned over and kissed him again.

"That's the last time I'm doing that," she said, pulling away. "The next time will be on you."

"I'm old enough to—"

"Be my father," she said, interrupting him. "We had this discussion before. Only from a chronological standpoint. From a maturity level, I'm up a few points and you're down a few, so that closes the gap."

There wasn't much he could say to that so he didn't.

They met Pelton and Crome at Crome's place. Patricia and Darcy showed up soon after. The Peltons ordered pizzas and soft drinks for everyone and they ate until they were stuffed.

With the slug of pizza in his gut, Blu felt the need to visit the gym before his waist size grew. It seemed like the perfect time, except his truck was elsewhere and he was stuck.

While the group hung around on the back deck watching the waves, he and Tess took a walk on the beach to "get some exercise."

When they had walked far enough down the beach and were out of earshot of the others sitting on the back deck, Tess said, "You aren't going to keep coming up with reasons why this wouldn't work, are you?"

"No," he said. "But you know I'm committed to someone else, right?"

"I know you have an unanswered marriage proposal," she said. "Personally, I think she's had enough time to decide."

He said, "I do love her."

"Will you still love her if she says no?"

That was the question he'd been avoiding, the one he didn't want to have an answer for because he had all but convinced himself she would say yes.

"Up until today, I'd have answered that I wasn't sure what I'd do."

He watched her smile grow beneath her glasses. "So I've given you something else to think about?"

"You could say that," he said. "But I've been around a lot longer than you. It's never all sunshine and roses. I've got a daughter and an ex-wife."

"You think I'm a virgin?" she asked.

If he answered yes, she'd know he was lying. And if he answered no, she might not like that one, either.

Before he could come up with a reply that wouldn't get him into trouble, she said, "I'm sorry. That was an unfair question. And, by the way, you did so well in recognizing the hazards of answering it. The other men I've dated would have either lied or upset me."

"With age comes wisdom," he said.

"And a little slice of ego."

He stopped and they faced each other. "Overconfidence is one of the things that's kept me alive this long."

"Sounds like a lecture coming on," she said, now with a hint of annoyance in her voice.

"No lecture," he said. "I believe you understand that I have one of those jobs where I can go to work in the morning and not come home alive in the evening."

Breaking her own protocol, she moved in close and gave him a hug. "I know."

As if knowing it was about to get more serious, Patricia sent a text saying they had a break with one of Crome's neighbors thanks to Darcy. There was footage of the beach area in front of Crome's house. And whatever she and Blu were doing, they needed to stop and come back. Apparently nobody at the table bought their excuse to walk off dinner.

Chapter Thirty-Five

Crome eyed Blu upon his return with Tess, but didn't have any energy to spare on giving him a hard time about it.

The hero neighbor was next door and had an arsenal as well as his entire property covered with cameras. They extended to the beach area, a tad farther out than necessary for home security in Crome's opinion. If he didn't need to see what was in the footage, he might have labeled the guy, an overweight white man in his forties, as a pervert. Or more specifically, a Peeping Tom.

Crome wasn't the only one who'd picked up on it. Patricia, Darcy, and Tess were visibly creeped out by their good Samaritan.

He, on the other hand, seemed to be getting a little too much pleasure in having flesh and blood females in his fortress domicile. The beachfront property the guy owned meant that he was well off. Even if he had bought it cheap twenty years ago, the taxes on it at the present time alone would bankrupt most Americans.

Tess had written down the times the phone number in question had been found by the FBI to be on while at Crome's address.

She said, "Crome, lemme see your phone."

Crome handed it over. She scrolled through the recent calls, found what Crome thought was the time of his call, and told the peeper.

He worked the mouse, found the time, and played the footage.

Everyone in the room watched the screen and the camera's eerie fixation on women in bikinis. It was as if it had a mind of its own, or, more accurately, was being controlled.

Crome caught the image of a man who stood up from underneath a colorful umbrella, closed it, picked it up, and carried it and a bag away. It was about the right time.

Blu said, "You all see that?"

"That's him," Crome said. He referred to the similarity between the man on the screen and the man on the video footage from the marina and Myrtle Beach.

Tess gave the peeper a wide-eyed smile, even more pronounced and flirty than the one she used in her segments. "Do you have any cameras that might track where that man goes?"

"Sure do," the peeper said.

The man was quite proud of his miniature Big Brother set-up. Even if he used it primarily to leer at unsuspecting women.

Crome had the feeling that once they had gotten what they needed, the man would be exposed for what he was. And he didn't feel bad about it.

Blu watched the footage, his frustration rising. Each time, the man walked outside the view of the camera, or the peeper had moved the camera to focus on some woman's cleavage.

On video time-stamped four days ago, the cameras were left to roll and the man stayed in focus all the way around the house to his parked SUV out front. The SUV had a different license plate than what the group had recorded up to this point.

Blu, with the help of his daughter, had been learning how to use the access his PI license gave him to do his own DMV searches. Gladys, his DMV contact, would not continue to work there forever so he needed a long-term plan. Hope had proven more than proficient enough to help him.

Patricia had called her niece, Josie, to come over to her house on Montague where the group convened after leaving the peeper.

The general consensus was they all felt like they needed bleach baths to wash the creepiness of that guy off. Crome had made an offhand comment about using the cameras for target practice. Blu had a feeling that Folly Beach Police would get an anonymous tip about them. With the ability to spy on people like that, there was no limit to what the man might try, and it was best to put him out of business.

Josie set Blu up on her aunt's computer and helped access the DMV records. Together they did a search on the abductor's plate number.

The address that came up was another anomaly. Out of concern for moderation, Blu did not want Crome or Pelton to go roaring off, guns drawn, again.

And he didn't want to put any of the women in danger.

Under protest from both Crome and Pelton, Blu called Powers and asked how he felt about doing a little moonlighting for Blu Carraway Investigations. He'd done it before, albeit a long time ago.

Luckily, Darcy Pelton managed to talk her husband off the proverbial ledge.

Unfortunately there was no one in the room who could get through to Crome. He was targeted first with the abduction of Maureen. Harmony and the mayor were another story, and it no longer made sense to Blu that this was solely about Crome.

Of course, no one could tell Crome that, at least in a way that he would listen.

Powers, perhaps from having twenty years of added wisdom, declined to be directly involved. He again offered the two patrol units but Blu didn't want to spook their suspect by any visible police presence.

Faced with no other options, Blu went solo. He could have satiated his own controlling nature by giving Crome a bunch of rules he needed to follow. However, Crome was selective with what rules he followed under normal circumstances. Kidnap his girlfriend and the number of rules governing his actions dropped to zero.

The address was a home in a North Mount Pleasant subdivision off of Seventeen toward Georgetown. The homes were around twenty years old and the neighborhood was well-maintained. With the influx of new business in the Charleston area, all real estate benefited. This neighborhood was no exception. It also helped that Charleston consistently rated as one of the top cities in the U.S., if not the world, to move to.

And Blu Carraway Investigations benefited along with the growth. Unbeknownst to Crome, Blu had accepted Adam Kincaid's offer to keep the investigation agency on retainer, hence the trip to South America with Jennifer Kincaid and her friends. It was a mid-five-figure job for two weeks' worth of work. Blu misled—okay, lied to—Crome by not telling him about the extended contract. As far as he knew, it was a one-time gig and didn't come with strings. Crome never could handle strings. If he could, Crome would have been with Maureen and maybe prevented her from getting taken. This all rattled around Blu's head as he contemplated their next moves.

Given the seriousness of the situation with Maureen and Harmony, Blu could not risk dredging the gutter and maybe killing the wrong person.

Chapter Thirty-Six

Crome was ticked off. Blu had made a call and was gone, not telling him anything. Tess and Darcy left, too, going somewhere they also didn't disclose. Plus, his bike was on the other side of town. He said, "Come on, kid."

"Where to?" Pelton asked, but Crome knew the kid didn't care as long as it was in pursuit of violence.

"Well, right now you can take me back to my bike and check on your bar."

Pelton seemed visibly disappointed.

"And then," Crome said, "you can buy me a cup of coffee."

"Gee," Pelton said, "can I pump your gas and wax your Harley, too?"

"No need to get all sensitive now."

Pelton walked to the door. "You coming or not?"

Crome needed to get back to working alone.

And then Patricia said, "I'm coming with you."

Crome would have rather she stayed.

Before he could object, Pelton said, "Normally I'd say no, but I don't want to be looking for three missing women. Two's more than enough."

The kid was right. But Crome still needed to ditch them. Patricia would be safe with Pelton in his bar.

Tess watched Darcy work, first talking to several sources using her Jeep's Bluetooth, and then stopping at what had to be the worst dive in the lowcountry. Brack's wife had asked her to come along and curiosity more than anything else had prompted her to say yes.

When Darcy parked in front of the dilapidated building on the west side of town, Tess had a feeling she should know about this place. She asked, "Is this where Crome and Harmony found Tim, the drug dealer who shot her last year?"

"Yes." Darcy put the SUV into park, got out, and waited for Tess.

Tess had the feeling that Darcy was one of those people who worked extremely efficiently and did not waste steps or words. If Tess did not want to be left behind, she needed to keep up.

Before they got to the door, Tess recognized the song playing in the bar. It was Foreigner's "Dirty White Boy." Her parents were Generation Xers and listened to eighties music all the time. She'd been force-fed classic rock her entire life.

They entered the derelict bar. Dim lighting and worn linoleum greeted them and Tess found herself realizing there were no windows in the place. She loved living in Charleston. There was so much scenery that she could never get enough. It was one of the reasons she found herself attracted to Blu. The way he lived—his island—told her he was a potential soul mate. Sitting on his porch overlooking the marsh and his horses at dawn or dusk was some of the best viewing in the lowcountry.

Inside the bar the scenery was another version of lowcountry wildlife, rundown forty-year-olds with addiction issues and felony records.

Next to these lost souls, she and Darcy stood out. Instead of dingy jeans and soiled t-shirts covering middle-aged stagnation, the women were brightly clothed, tanned, and slender.

Darcy avoided the half dozen men seated around the bar and went to the one pouring the drinks.

Tess had to really strain her memory to come up with what she remembered about the place. Crome and Harmony had come here looking for a drug dealer named Tim who had information on a missing stripper. Harmony had been upset because Crome had gone around her and gotten the tip from Darcy, and shown up mad and emotional. Crome managed to get into a bar fight with the owner and two others and ended up killing Tim the drug dealer. But not before Harmony had been shot. Overall it had been a big mess.

What happened afterward was what Tess struggled to recall. It was something about Darcy's source being another bartender that worked in the place. The same one that eventually bought it after the previous owner went to jail for pulling a shotgun on Crome and shooting one of his bar patrons in the kneecap. The victim of the shooting would walk with a limp for the rest of his life which would be less than five years if he didn't change his lifestyle.

The man Darcy spoke with now, a thirty-something-year-old African American named Derek with a stylish afro and trimmed beard, medium-dark skin, and a toned build over a six-foot frame, was her original source. He was also the bar's new owner.

Some people in a similar position might not appreciate being seen talking to two semi-retired news correspondents. They might be afraid of being labeled as snitches. Derek was not one of them. From what Tess knew about him, he had started with nothing in a North Charleston slum and had survived by learning the right information was worth something.

Darcy had done a segment on gang activity and had stumbled across Derek as she worked the story. He knew a lot about what went on in Charleston County. When Darcy wanted to find an answer to Crome's question about Tim who supplied low-end strippers with coke, she knew to call Derek. And he knew who she was talking about.

What Derek got out of the arrangement was a little hazy.

After Darcy had finished and they were outside again in the lowcountry oven, Tess asked, "Why's he a source?"

"What do you mean?"

"I mean what does he get out of it? You're a married, uppity white chick who isn't known to stray. He's risking a lot just to talk to you."

Darcy gave Tess a weak smile. "When I worked for Patricia, I didn't care about anything but getting to the bottom of the story. I have a lot of money, something most of my colleagues don't have. And I wasn't afraid to pay well for information."

"So Derek's on your payroll?"

"In a roundabout sort of way."

Tess waited.

Darcy said, "He has a special needs son. I got him into a program."

"And Derek feels obligated to help."

"Yes."

Normal people might call that a bribe. But Tess and Darcy were not normal. They both lived for the story. Investigative reporting was tough and most of the people who liked to talk never told the truth. It was a rare thing when they could get someone who knew the truth to speak it. And Derek's son was now getting the help he needed.

"What did he have to say?" she asked.

Darcy unlocked the doors of her Jeep with the key fob. "We're in trouble. I'll tell you when we're inside."

They got in and Darcy rubbed her eyes with a hand. Tess noticed a worry line just off-center of the pretty woman's forehead. Harmony and she and Tess were pretty much equals, all things considered. Each had their high points.

But Darcy was the whole package. Beautiful, ambitious, rich, worldly, connected, and married to the catch of the lowcountry. Nearly every single woman wanted Brack and to most of them it really didn't matter that he was married. Tess and Harmony spent many a Saturday evenings in his bar flirting with him, and Darcy knew it.

The time Harmony and Tess got drunk with Crome and Blu, and Brack invited them all back to his house, was something she would never forget. Most men, if they were able to get drunk versions of Tess and Harmony corralled in their homes, would be working angles to get one or both of them into bed, but Brack invited them back to his house where he and his wife lived.

Blu was sort of an older version of Brack, except that he wasn't. Blu wasn't married, which was why Tess felt it was now or never.

Darcy closed her door and pressed the start button. The V-8 engine in her SUV rumbled to life. She turned the air conditioner on max and stretched out her hands to capture the blowing air.

Tess said, "How are we in trouble?"

"Word through the underworld is someone is giving Blu and Crome a hard time. They don't know why, but they are waiting to see what happens. Some of them are even cheering it on."

"What else did he say?"

"That this wasn't about drugs or strippers or prostitutes or any of Blu's current high-dollar clients. Derek's almost positive about that. He figures he would have heard more if that were the case. So that leaves something that happened in the past of Blu Carraway Investigations, either with Crome or Blu."

"But why Harmony?" Tess asked.

"Why Maureen?" Darcy said.

Tess didn't understand and Darcy must have read it on her face.

"Neither woman is part of the distant past of Blu or Crome."

"Crome and Maureen were an item a few years ago, before Crome took his three-year sabbatical."

"I thought about that," Darcy said. "But I think she was chosen because it would cause Crome heartache today."

Tess nodded, understanding where Darcy was going with the thought. "The guy got cocky after he was able to take Maureen and not get caught. The next target would be us or Billie. Oh my—" She interrupted herself and dug into her purse.

Darcy said, "I've already called Billie and told her to be careful."

"Good," Tess said.

"So tell me," Darcy said, "is that why you're moving in on Blu?"

Chapter Thirty-Seven

Friday evening

The question caught Tess off guard. It was blunt, on point, and not filtered.

"That's really none of your business." It came out more like a huff and Tess, already irritated, now found herself upset at how she wasn't able to handle Darcy's question about her intention.

"You're right," Darcy said. "What I've seen, Blu is a good man. Billie is a good woman. The fact that she hasn't given him an answer could be a lot of things. It could be because she doesn't want to marry him. It could be because she's dealing with her sick mother, or it could be a side of her we haven't seen, a cruel side. I'm not sure which and I think Blu is struggling with it as well. This abduction, as sick as it sounds, is probably a good distraction for him. Otherwise the man might be approaching a breaking point."

"You're trying to say I'm not helping him, is that right?" The irritation was front and center and focused on Darcy. Who did she think she was?

Why the hell hadn't Billie called? Or, maybe the question Blu should ask himself is why he hadn't called her lately. Was it because he was upset that she didn't immediately say yes when he asked her to marry him? Now he was tempted to get involved with a woman twenty years younger. His daughter would have a fit. He'd lose

Billie forever.

It hadn't helped that the address he'd gone to track down was worthless. Another rabbit hole that ended up at an assisted living community where none of the residents drove. With nothing else to do, he doubled back to Patricia's house.

In her kitchen, he felt an arm across his back and turned to find Patricia standing next to him. They stood there like that, her arm on his back.

She rested her head on his shoulder. "I'm worried about my girl."

He felt like such a dolt.

Harmony used to work for Patricia who had a reputation of treating her employees like her kids since she didn't have any. Harmony was like a daughter to her and she'd been taken.

He put his arm around her. "We're going to find her."

She raised her head and looked at him. "You promise?"

He looked into her eyes. "I promise." And the man who had taken the women would die. Either by his hand or Crome's. He made that promise to himself but wouldn't say it aloud.

"And if he harmed her?"

"I'll take him apart inch by inch."

She returned her head to his shoulder. "I want to watch."

The only thing that wasn't fun about this whole situation to the man was that he couldn't be a fly on the wall around Mick Crome and Blu Carraway. He was quite sure they were going nuts. They had a reputation of getting the job done, even the most difficult job. And it had been five days since he'd taken Maureen.

Maybe he was too good. It wasn't even close. He could kill the women, dump them in the ocean, and go back to his normal life and no one would ever know what he had done.

But he didn't want that. When this was over, he wanted Mick Crome and Blu Carraway to know exactly what he had done, what he had gotten away with, and why. And he wanted them to know it the very moment he shot them in their heads.

The problem, he realized, was he was losing his patience—losing his edge.

If that happened to any significant degree, he would lose the game. He did not want to lose the game. Never, never, never.

What he needed was to eliminate any paper trail linking him and her to Blu Carraway Investigations. Carraway was not computer savvy—he was old school. Old School meant paper. It meant client files.

So far Carraway and Crome hadn't made the connection, even when the mayor washed up on the beach. While killing him was not part of the original plan, it was a bonus. That man had deserved to die, too. Truth be told, he was the cause of the whole thing and being able to get rid of him in the process was pure gold.

But now the man needed to get the files.

Chapter Thirty-Eight

Saturday morning
DAY SIX

A break gave Blu time to think. He finally had to admit to himself that his nerves were shot. It took a lot of effort not to think about all the terrible things that could be happening to Maureen and Harmony. There wasn't much left in him and he knew he was running on fumes.

Pelton had said. "Darcy's source says there's no way it could be from anything recent. The word is that the target is your agency."

"But why Maureen?"

"She was the easiest and it took Crome out early."

He was right. If it had been Billie, he would have been a basket case and Crome would have torn up the town. By taking out Crome first, it changed the dynamics of how they reacted. Blu knew he was slower and more methodical than Crome. That's what the kidnapper wanted. He knew how they operated and knew which play to make to predict the outcome. And it worked beautifully.

This meant, again, it was either a previous client or someone they burned for a previous client. But they weren't back to square one anymore. The answer was in the files of all the previous clients.

*   *   *

Saturday morning

The man parked off the road just down from the small bridge connecting Blu's island to the mainland. Given the lack of any fencing, he wondered how the horses never ended up wandering down the road and getting hit by a car. There were other homes scattered here and there, but he supposed even if the horses did wander, there wasn't enough traffic to pose much of a threat.

In a shoulder holster underneath a lightweight jogging jacket was a Magnum forty-four. It would take out an engine block at a hundred feet. He wanted as much firepower heading onto enemy territory as he could carry.

Having seen no one pass by in the last five minutes, the man walked up to the bridge, looked around one last time, and crossed onto the island. It was eerily silent. A mosquito tagged him in the neck. He swatted at it, but three more showed up. The bugs were terrible and he wondered how anyone could live here.

In addition to the forty-four, he also packed serious bug repellant which he reapplied. Ever since he'd been a kid, the bloodsuckers had feasted on him with an unrelenting madness. It had kept him indoors most of his life, his parents choosing to stay in the lowcountry cesspool instead of moving inland where the bugs were less a pestilence. That was another reason to dislike them.

His parents had shown him that they cared more about themselves than him. Later in his life, he'd shown them how much he appreciated their selfishness. He was proud of the fact that he would not have to care for them in their twilight years. He'd already taken care of that with a heavy dose of carbon monoxide while they slept. What he hadn't counted on was the inheritance. Evidently Daddy had been pretty good with money. After the police ruled it an accident when their investigation turned up a leaking furnace, he'd solemnly accepted the seven-figure check minus estate taxes and semi-retired.

Hands down that was the best decision of his life. It gave him the time he needed to work on his passion and also plan revenge on his enemies, Blu Carraway and his Neanderthal partner being at the top of the list.

He thought about this as he walked, forgetting he needed to be aware of his surroundings.

His plan unraveled before his eyes as three horses stepped out from the palmetto trees in front of him at the same time a shriek from behind made him jump.

He managed to slip out the long-barreled forty-four without fumbling. The problem was that the shriek had been really loud and really close. Meaning the distance between him and the animal was just a few feet.

As he spun around to shoot, the black horse charged him. He raised the pistol in time for the horse to crash into him, knocking him over and the gun out of his hand. The man went flying one way and his gun went the other way.

He hit the ground hard. Thanks to adrenaline, he got to his feet quick and found out the horse had turned around to charge him again.

With no weapon, a wall of now five horses blocking his path to the house, and the charging black stallion, his only option was retreat, which he did, running as fast as he'd ever run in his life.

And then he felt a sharp pain in his buttocks just as his foot touched the bridge. He kept running and didn't stop, making it all the way back to his truck without any more bites.

He got in his truck and slammed the door. The horse had not followed him that far. He massaged the area where he'd felt the pain and looked at his hand. There was no blood. The horse had nipped him through his clothes but had not broken skin. He'd have a bruise.

Somehow, Carraway's horses had the island zeroed in to prevent any unwelcome guests. He loved most wildlife but he'd been outsmarted by a group of demon-possessed animals.

He started his SUV, put it in drive, and idled up the road.

When he got to the bridge that led to Carraway's island home, he noted the black horse standing guard as if making sure he did not return. He stepped on the gas and got out of there.

Saturday, noon

Carraway would never understand how the new but scuffed forty-four Magnum found its way onto his doorstep. He looked down at the weapon and then scanned the area. Nothing was out of place. Several horses grazed on the marsh grass. Another drank from the water trough. Dink and Doofus had stood guard, awaiting the cover charge of produce, which Blu promptly paid.

Murder had greeted him at the bridge, more like he stood as if at post. When Blu approached, the horse didn't move right away.

Blu had leaned out his truck window, honked the horn, and said, "Come on, now."

Murder gave him a neigh and then stepped aside to let him through.

Blu had come to an understanding with the horses. They agreed not to coat the gravel drive with manure and he agreed to always have fresh water and food reserves if the weather got too cold or too hot. It seemed to be working okay for both parties.

Without knowing where to go next, and not wanting to go to a bar or home, Crome found himself riding toward his business partner's house. As he idled to a stop close to the front door, Dink and Doofus greeted him. They normally greeted everyone, but they had taken a liking to Crome. He always had something for them and made sure he gave them each nose rubs.

While handing out the treats, Crome felt someone looking at him and turned to find Blu sitting on the steps to his house. His hands were covered in latex gloves and held a Magnum forty-four in one of them.

"Where'd you get the cannon?" Crome asked, knowing Blu preferred nine millimeters as well.

"It was on my steps right where I'm sitting when I got home."

"No kidding." No one had ever dropped off any firearms at Crome's house.

Blu held it up, angling it in his hand. "Looks brand new except for some scratches on the metal, like someone had dropped it."

"Why the gloves?"

"Something doesn't seem right."

Crome walked to him and propped a foot on the step next to Blu. "You mean besides the free gun?"

"For starters," Blu said and aimed the gun in the direction of the black horse that was grazing in the marsh grass, "Murder was standing on the island side of the bridge when I drove up. And he looked even more pissed off than usual."

Crome stared at the horse. "You don't say?" There had always been something about Murder that demanded respect. No one ever knew if and when the horse would snap. Maybe someone uninvited had come and pressed the right button and got a taste of how crazy that horse was.

"And," Blu continued, "I had to honk my horn to get him to snap out of whatever zone he was in, recognize me, and reluctantly clomp out of the way. I tell you, I half expected him to charge my truck, he looked so mad."

Crome chuckled. "You know, most horses get spooked. You got yourself a real sentry, there. And, if you don't mind me sayin', I think you named him appropriately."

"That's not the strangest part," Blu said. "This gun is." He raised it up again so Crome could see it. "Based on its condition, it looks like someone flung it across my gravel driveway."

"Yes it does," Crome had to agree.

"If that were the case, I would have found it there."

And then it hit Crome what Blu had said. "You found it on the steps?"

"Right here."

Crome pulled out his vape pen and took a drag. Exhaling, he said, "It's just a hunch, but I would say that if you tested that gun for DNA, you'd find horse saliva on it."

Blu stood. "That's exactly what I was thinking."

"Okay," Crome said, "we'll deal with who the owner of the gun could be in a minute. First, let's be clear on what we're saying. We're saying we believe your horse scared someone off your property, found the gun they dropped, put it on the step for you to find, and then stood guard until you got home. That's what we're saying, right?"

Blu said, "That's what we're saying."

"Jesus," Crome said.

"Now," Blu said, putting a hand on Crome's shoulder, "about who the owner of the gun could be."

Crome nodded. "It's him."

Blu took out his phone.

Crome listened as his partner spoke with Detective Powers, rattling off the serial number, and then requesting the police examine it for any kind of evidence including DNA. While it would be interesting to find out there was actual horse saliva residue, the more important information would be any other DNA or prints, like the kidnapper's. If they could get something to identify the kidnapper from the gun, they'd be back in the game and the guy would be dead before the sun went down.

After he and Crome checked the house, clearing all the rooms and doing a thorough examination to make sure nothing had been disturbed, Blu fed the horses all the produce from his house. If his hunch was correct, they deserved the reward for protecting their home. Not only would he never accuse them of freeloading again, he would talk to a local vet about how to care for them in a way that wouldn't spook them. It wasn't as if the horses would let a stranger approach, and might get violent if they felt threatened. Murder had all but proven he could be vicious. What Blu was interested in was a way to check them out to determine if they needed anything to stay healthy. He had no idea, aside from giving them water and produce and hay, what to do with them. But he was now ready to call them his.

Chapter Thirty-Nine

Saturday, early afternoon

In the bathroom mirror, the man had lowered his pants and underwear and found a dark bruise on his right butt cheek. He still could not believe how he'd fooled everyone—Mick Crome, Blu Carraway, Patricia Voyels, Brack Pelton, Darcy Pelton, and Tess Ray—only to be outsmarted by a horse.

One that he hoped he'd never have to see again. The animal, he was now convinced, was possessed. Not many people, much less animals, could have come up with and executed a plan like that. What kind of creatures were these?

In fact, why were they attacking him? He'd spent his life fighting for them. And this was how they repaid him?

He shuddered at the thought of what could have happened— namely that the animals could have trampled him to death—and held an ice pack to his bruise, walking around his house half naked to the kitchen.

Up to this point, the only animals he disliked were dogs. One had bit him at an early age and he'd hated them ever since. Now it appeared he'd have to add horses to the list.

If he couldn't get into Carraway's house, then he had to make the P.I. think that this had to do with something else, derail him until it was time to reveal it all to him just before he and Crome died.

The drive back from Carraway's house had given him time to

think. He'd settled on two options. Both were dangerous and could blow up in his face. But if he succeeded, Carraway would have to go down another rabbit hole.

Saturday, early afternoon

Crome memorized the serial number of the forty-four before Powers bagged and took it. Even the detective couldn't believe the story about Murder the horse. It was definitely one for the books.

He had someone of his own who could look up the serial number. Ten years ago, on a job, Crome had run into a couple of agents in the F.B.I. and not the garden variety kind. Crome's job was to stop a husband from violating the restraining order his wife had against him. The man was connected and had foot soldiers who would not mind taking someone like Crome off the board if he got in their way.

The man, unfortunately for him, was also on the F.B.I. watch list. The agents Crome had run across initially did not like him getting in their way. After a talk with the agents, with Crome giving them his intel on the man's gambling habit and who his bookie was, something only a few people knew about, they figured Crome knew what he was doing.

Since their job was only surveillance while Crome's could best be described as discouragement, they agreed to work together. Crome knew their motive in letting him in was to rattle the target and maybe get him to slip up.

It worked out well initially. Crome beat up the three henchmen closest to the target and had a discussion with the man that may or may not have included a few broken fingers. But instead of listening to reason as explained to him by Crome, he elected to send more men after him. The agents, having the man's place wired in, got evidence of him placing the hit on Crome. Conspiracy to commit murder was more than enough to send him away for a long time. Of course, a man like that could not do hard time. So he turned snitch and the agents got the whole ring, five other bosses. Crome's client got her peace because the feds relocated the man to the other side of the country.

Those same feds were still working cases. Crome hadn't contacted them in a while, but the last time he did they'd been helpful. He decided to give them a shot.

From memory, Crome dialed a number that went to voicemail. He gave his name and phone number and hung up.

An hour later, his phone buzzed.

He answered with, "Yo."

"Is this Mick Crome?"

"Who's asking?"

"What do you want?"

No pleasantries, but these men were not into that. They were into nailing criminals.

Crome said, "Can you run the serial number of a forty-four Magnum for me?"

"What is it?"

He rattled off the number, again from memory. One thing Crome had was a mind for information retention.

"Give me a few hours," the man said.

"Thanks."

The call ended.

Chapter Forty

Darcy, Tess, and Patricia arrived at their destination. Tess knew having Patricia in the car put both of her ex-reporters in a difficult position. One woman asking questions was best. Two of them were not as effective, but safer. Three of them were at least one too many.

And the way it was, none of them felt it was okay to leave someone in the car while two worked a source. Hence the three of them approached the source together in the upstairs bar that served three-hundred-dollar cocktails.

This source was Tess' and he was a twenty-something broker for one of the big investment firms. He'd tried to woo her with confidential information which blew up in his face when she took the intel but rejected his proposition.

Their target, with hair slightly disheveled and a wrinkled collar on his polo, eyed them with red cheeks and a goofy grin. Clearly the drink in front of him had not been his first.

A waitress came over to the four-top table now filled with the young man and three women. She greeted all three women by name. Such was the clout they held.

Tess ordered a Coke Zero, Darcy a water, and Patricia a club soda.

Tess said, "Thanks for meeting with us, John."

He picked up his glass, looked at the liquid and ice, and said, "Did I have a choice?"

"Sure," Tess said, "you could not talk and maybe cause Harmony to be missing for longer than if you did."

With a jerk of his head, he eyed her. "That's not even fair."

Patricia asked, "What did you and Harmony talk about that had her meeting with the mayor?"

"Am I going to get compensated for losing my job?" he asked.

"Did you get fired?" Tess asked.

"Not yet," he said. "But meeting the three of you in the open like this, I'm as good as gone."

"I know all your bosses," Patricia said.

"And they know you," he said.

She didn't let up. "One call and you become untouchable."

"You'd do that for me?" he asked, not really sounding like he was buying what she was selling.

"You give us what you gave Harmony and I promise I'll do whatever I can to make sure you don't lose your job."

The truth was, and the guy probably knew it, he would still be tainted. They might not fire him right away, but his days would be numbered. Patricia hob-knobbed with the most powerful men in Charleston, but none of them wanted one of her moles working in their camp.

"I'm sure you will." It didn't sound like he believed what he said.

"So what've you got?" Tess asked.

The man's brown eyes were hazy, but got a little focused when he said, "The mayor wasn't just a horny old man, if you know what I mean."

"Enlighten us," Tess said.

He took another drink from his three-figure highball and set the glass down. "Remember when talk of the cruise ships coming to town started?"

"I was ten," Darcy said. "But I remember before he was mayor, Ron Jansen was a proponent."

"What's your point?" Tess asked.

The man looked at them all, one at a time, with lazy eyes. "Are all three of you going to fire questions at me?"

Even in his drunken state, Tess realized he was right. "I'll ask the questions."

"Gee, thanks," he said. "I feel so much better now."

What he said almost made Tess smile. She was probably the most difficult of the three. Not because she was mean, but because she always meant business. Harmony had learned to manipulate men. Tess interrogated. In the end, people had told Patricia that after an interview with her, they needed a stiff drink.

"Again, what's your point?" Tess asked.

"My firm handles—handled—the mayor's personal finances. During the time the decision was made to accept the larger cruise ships into Charleston, he got a significant amount of money."

"Illegally?"

"Now," the man said, "how would I know that? All I know is we put it into play and made him a hell of a return."

"So you're saying you think he took a bribe?" Tess asked.

Tess wanted to know why there was even a bribe offered. Charleston the city, if not all of its residents, wanted the revenue the patrons of the tour ships would provide.

"No," he said. "I'm telling you to go back to when the cruise ship concept was in its infancy, just before the Cruise Vessel Act of 2000."

"The mayor, even before he was mayor, supported the cruise ships," Tess said.

Jingling the ice in his glass, John said, "He was the leading advocate in Charleston. And my firm began to handle his personal finances way back then."

"How far back?"

"From 2000."

Nodding, Tess said, "So the windfall after the decision was just the final payoff."

"Yes," he said, "and it was huge."

Patricia said, "He always did play the long game."

*   *   *

Saturday six p.m.

Blu and Crome sat on chairs on the front porch, slightly unmotivated because the gun serial number was a bust from both sources. They watched the Jeep Grand Cherokee pull to a stop in the gravel drive.

Before the women could get out, Dink and Doofus were on the scene.

Tess exited the Jeep with a grocery bag. She handed Patricia and Darcy carrots. Three more horses showed up and each got a carrot. They were getting tamer and bolder. Maybe they were tired of seeing Dink and Doofus get all the snacks and wanted some of their own.

Blu glanced around to make sure Murder wasn't close by. Just because he had proven himself a unique watch dog didn't mean he wouldn't trample the women. He found the black horse by the water trough. The horse, in Blu's opinion, knew everything going on. It was as if Murder allowed things to happen on his island.

Crome, holding a cup of coffee in one hand, waved to the women with the other. He didn't look well. Blu thought his friend was unraveling even more.

It had been six days since Maureen had been taken.

Tess approached the men, nodded at Blu, and stooped down and gave Crome a hug. The strength these women showed was impressive. Crome, a seasoned biker and killer, was about to come apart at the seams and these women, with two of their own in only God knows what kind of condition, were standing tall.

Blu wondered which one was going to be the spokeswoman.

Before Blu could ask, the sound that only a barely muffled V-8 engine could make rumbled into the drive. Pelton pulled to a stop next to his wife's Jeep and got out of his car. He had on a Black Flag t-shirt, which impressed Blu, along with his cargo shorts and sandals. His dog jumped out after him and went to sniffing around.

Dink and Doofus, undaunted as usual, finished their carrots and trotted up to the mutt.

They all seemed to get into a sniffing contest, Shelby sniffing at the horses' hooves and the horses stooping down to sniff the dog.

Doofus gave the dog a lick on his head, and Shelby gave him a friendly bark in return. The three of them then ran off, the dog keeping up with the horses around the house and into the marsh grass.

Pelton said, "I hope you have an outside shower."

In fact, Blu did. He'd installed it so that he and Billie could shower off after the boat rides they used to take to the barrier islands around the lowcountry coast, before he asked her to marry him and she ran away.

Darcy said, "Shelby never has problems making friends."

"So what's up?" Pelton asked.

Darcy asked Blu, "Did you have anything to do with the cruise ship lines coming to Charleston?"

It was an odd question. A lot of people made a lot of money from it, but not Blu Carraway Investigations.

"No."

"What about a client involved with it?"

Blu had an epiphany. It all came back to him—the woman shot to death in Battery Park with no leads, the job with Ron Jansen. How could he have been so stupid as to dismiss it?

He turned to Crome and said, "Remember Grietje?"

Crome said. "Jesus."

Blu said, "We keep coming back to a past client. I only had one that I remember that had dealings with the cruise ships. It was Ron Jansen."

Tess said, "We need to go back through your files on that job. Where do you keep them?"

"The complete set is in storage in West Ashley," Blu said. "I have some here inside but not that file."

Tess said, "We need to see it."

Chapter Forty-One

Saturday seven p.m.

Since getting in the house was a bust, the man decided to target the files in storage. Luckily, there was another unit just down from Carraway's that was available. And the place was old school, requiring the renters to supply their own padlocks instead of a more modern, keypad activated system. One set of bolt cutters would take care of the lock on Carraway's unit. The man knew he'd be on film, but if he covered his face, they wouldn't know who he was.

The tricky part was the vehicle. The place allowed the renters to pull their cars up to their units to unload or load. He'd need to do this to carry out the plan. But he needed a vehicle that couldn't be linked to him. Hence, he needed to steal another. The last time, he'd gotten lucky. Instead of leaving their pet dog at home like they should have, the morons left the car running with the air blowing so their beloved pooch wouldn't suffer from the heat. Prime pickin's, as his grandmother used to say. Pop the lock, dump the dog, which was a small reward in and of itself, and he was gone.

This time he trolled the local big box store lot for a vehicle suitable for the task. His requirements were simple: old enough not to have an alarm but nice enough not to be noticeable. Something around twenty years old was perfect, and given that there were a lot of people still suffering from the crash of 2008, there were a lot of older cars on the road. Who could afford a new one when the income wasn't there?

And then he found what he was looking for. A Ford Ranger from the early nineties. It was perfect. Faded paint but still decent. He parked on the opposite side of the lot, strolled down the sidewalk in front of all the small businesses also renting space in the shopping plaza, walked into the big store on one side and out the other. The Ranger was still there but he felt he had to work fast. The lock popped quick and he opened the door. It was clean and smelled like air fresheners. He guessed it was a little old lady's ride.

The automatic transmission confirmed his guess. Most of these small trucks back then had manuals, from what he remembered. He hot-wired it and the engine kicked over. He slid to the passenger's side, propped a foot on the wheel, and used all his strength to break the steering interlock. When it popped, he slid back, put it in reverse, and backed out of the spot.

Saturday, seven p.m.

Harmony couldn't see Maureen, but hoped she was close by. The room she'd been locked in had its own bathroom, but there was only one door and it was locked on the outside with a round plate covering where the knob would be inside the room.

There were also cameras in opposite corners of the room. She'd once tried to cover them but "he" came in soon after, slapped her across the face so hard she saw stars, and uncovered them. After that, she wanted nothing more than to put him out of his misery. It only occurred to her in a vague notion that he hadn't violated her physically and she was grateful of that. But the threat was there all the time. He could do whatever he wanted to. He was stronger and he had her locked up. She relied on him for food and water. There was a faucet and commode in the bathroom, but he could cut the water to the place at any time.

The room had no windows. It had no furniture. Nothing but a

sleeping bag and pillow on the floor. The bathroom had cheap soap and shampoo, a toothbrush and toothpaste, a washcloth, and towel. He'd taken her purse away and made her change into sweats and a t-shirt. Every day, he'd give her a fresh set. No shoes. No underwear. No makeup.

He had total control of her. He'd already violated her sense of security. If he ever decided to take the rest of her, there wasn't much she could do to stop him. She'd already made the decision that if he tried, she'd fight as if she were fighting for her life, which she would be. He would have to knock her unconscious or kill her. That would be the only way.

What bothered her the most was not knowing how to get in contact with Maureen. If Harmony managed to get out of the room, she'd know to look for the other woman. Her fear was that Maureen wouldn't know to do the same. She knew she had to get free first and get to Maureen.

The man pressed the remote control and watched as the garage door opened automatically. When the opening was big enough, he drove through, parked, and pressed the button to close the door. He didn't want any nosey neighbors to see what he was doing. In the bed of the truck, he loaded the boxes he'd prepped for this. It looked like he was just dropping off some things in his storage unit.

He thought about checking on the women, but decided he didn't have time. He needed to take care of the files and he needed to do that now.

Harmony heard the garage door open and steeled herself. The man didn't come to her room every time, but when he did it wasn't good. Instead, she focused her energy on a plan of escape. The room had no windows and no other doors. The one to the bathroom had been removed. All the vanity doors and drawers had also been removed. Even the mechanism that flushed the toilet had been removed. The man had shown her the way he wanted her to flush it—by filling a small, plastic trash can with water and pouring it down the commode. It would send the waste down the pipes.

The room had a light fixture that was mounted close to the ceiling and she had no way to reach it. The light switch cover was glued to the wall. In fact, all the electrical outlets had been blocked off and plastic plates had been glued over them. The carpet was really a rug that she could roll up, exposing bare concrete flooring. It was as if he'd spec'd the house to be able to jail people.

The only thing in the room that might have some use was the wood trim along the bottom edge of the wall. She'd worked on every corner and found one with a slight gap. It was all she had to work with, and since she had plenty of time, it was what she did. To avoid the watchful eyes of the cameras, she would shut the light off. The man had thought of a lot, but he hadn't thought of everything or he would have chained her to the wall.

Chapter Forty-Two

Blu parked in the lot in front of the storage center. It had been at least a year since he'd been here and he hoped he'd remember the lock combination. They exited the truck, went through the security gate and checked in at the front desk. The tattooed millennial working the counter barely looked up from his phone as they passed.

Crome slammed his hand down on the counter, startling Blu. "That out there's people's cherished stuff. Stuff they're paying you to watch over. If it wasn't important to them, they wouldn't." He pointed to the security monitors. "Watch those screens, not your phone. I come back here and find you doing anything but watching those screens, you and I are going to have a problem."

Blu looked at the screens. All the units had their numbers painted on them in big print so they were visible on the video. His number was two-five-eight. It was open. He took off running.

"Hey!" Crome called behind him.

Then he felt his partner on his heels.

His unit was a smaller one not too far from the front. He rounded a corner, saw the back of the pickup fifty feet ahead and the door to his unit still open. Someone wearing a mask that looked like a bad imitation of ex-Vice President Joe Biden stepped out, lit a rag with a lighter, and threw it inside the unit.

Before Blu could yell or do anything, a loud voom echoed down the corridor, followed by smoke and flames shooting out the opening.

On the other side of the flames, the figure got in the pickup and started to drive away.

Blu and Crome pulled out their guns and unloaded them into the exiting truck. It sped up and screeched around the corner.

They ran past the burning unit in pursuit of the truck, just in time to see it, the back of its cab full of holes and the back glass shot out, accelerate and crash through the wrought iron gate at a decent clip.

Blu and Crome ran back to the Xterra to give chase, but by the time Blu got on the road after the Ranger, it was gone. There were too many turns for it to take.

After about fifteen minutes, he gave up and went back to the storage lot. The fire department was there hosing down his unit, which was a complete loss.

In addition to the files, Blu kept a lot of mementos in the unit. One in particular came to mind: a picture of Hope at her third birthday party in Crome's arms along with a giant teddy bear.

The man had to steer the Ranger with one hand while he tried to stop the bleeding with his other. His right ear had been shot off and he was livid.

He managed to make it back to his house and get the garage door open. At the last minute, he decided to back the truck in thanks to a feeling it would not be good to have his nosy neighbors get a good look at the shot up back end of the truck. He pressed the button to close the door before he got out of the truck.

What was left of his ear was really bleeding. He cursed himself. First it was that damn horse, and then he has a run-in with Carraway and Crome at the very point he's most vulnerable. It was a good thing they didn't come five minutes earlier when he was pouring the cans of gasoline on everything in Blu's unit.

He stormed into his house and went right to his bathroom. Grabbing the first towel he found, he used it to try and stop the bleeding, his mind already working. He'd read in some magazine a while ago about ear reconstructive surgery and ear prosthetics. It wasn't the end of the world, but he would now have to plan on how to deal with his missing ear. Either a bullet or some of the glass from the back window had cut it off. Come to think of it, the back window did not shatter like safety glass. Someone had put in regular glass and now he had a missing ear because of it.

What was the world coming to?

He found gauze and medical tape in an old first aid kit and did his best to put pressure on the wound as he wound the tape around the gauze and his head several times. He finished, saw the gauze filling with blood but decided he couldn't do much more about it right now, and went to check on Harmony.

The lights were off in her room, something he'd noticed more and more lately. Before she'd started this, he could watch her for hours. Same with Maureen.

Truth be told, Maureen put up a better fight. The woman was bigger than Harmony and all those cases of beer she handled in her night job had given her considerable body strength. Before he'd been able to knock her out the last time, she managed a solid face punch that was so hard he'd seen stars. After that, he'd started drugging her food. He didn't want to deal with a sober and pissed off Maureen again.

Harmony hit like she'd been trained in aerobic kickboxing classes. It looked good, but it wasn't real fighting. He'd learned how to defend himself against three older cousins who all played football. Instead of protecting their nerdy younger cousin, they'd tormented him until he got even. At the time, he hated them, but they taught him how to street fight. To not back down and not stop until the other person was on the ground and bleeding.

And Harmony's light was still off. He'd put a stop to this, even if he had to hardwire the light to stay on all the time.

With his head no longer gushing blood down his neck, he put on the pair of leather gloves and brass knuckles he kept down the hall from the rooms his two guests stayed in.

The best video he'd watched was Harmony doing her exercise routine until she got so tired she passed out. With no concept of time, she must not have realized she had worked out for two and a half hours straight.

He approached her door, hoping she was asleep.

Harmony heard the garage door open again and heard the vehicle enter. Something seemed off, but she couldn't put her finger on it. What she could put her finger on was the piece of trim she'd managed to pull away from the wall, nails and all.

There was no going back this time. The man would see what she'd done and would not like it.

She listened for the slight shuffling of his feet down the hall moving toward her door. It was now or never.

The lock clicked and the door swung in, light blasting into the room momentarily blinding her. She'd forgotten about how her eyes had adjusted to the darkness.

The man opened the door, saw a lump in Harmony's sleeping bag, and stepped in, about to call out to her. And then the board came from out of nowhere and struck him in the face. Except it had a nail in it. He screamed and tried to pull the board away. The pain was so much more intense than what he felt when his ear got shot off.

But someone else pulled it away first, and it hurt worse being ripped out than when it hit him. Before he could scream, he saw the board come at him again.

He turned away, trying to avoid the end with the nail. Except the middle part that hit him this time also had a nail sticking out. It got him in the chest and he fell to the ground.

Harmony heard more than saw him fall.

Her eyes still mostly blinded, she pushed past him and made her way down the hall, screaming, "Maureen! Where are you? Maureen! Maureen!"

What she found instead of Maureen were the laundry room, the mud room, and a half-bathroom. It was the locked door that stopped her. And it wouldn't open.

Chapter Forty-Three

Detective Powers was on the scene of the torched storage unit by the time Blu and Crome returned. Blu explained what had happened and gave him the plate number for the truck. He would have tried to get something from Gladys, but it was after five and she would already be home from her job at the DMV.

Blu and Crome listened while Powers called it in.

The response that it had been stolen didn't surprise Blu. What did surprise him was that it had been stolen only two hours ago and from a place two blocks away.

Powers worked a judge over the phone and within five minutes had an approved court order to view all the camera footage from every business in the shopping center. An officer at the courthouse picked up the document from the judge and met them at the store twenty minutes later.

Having had the practice with Detective Wilson in Myrtle Beach for analyzing video, it didn't take Blu and Crome long to find the truck and the same man, who'd taken the other vehicles, stealing it too. Like in Myrtle Beach, they backtracked his footsteps and were almost stumped when they saw him come at the truck from the store exit.

Powers was the one who caught him entering the store with a group of shoppers. That took them half an hour, but it was a lucky break.

The problem was the big box store's footage did not extend to where he'd parked. They would have to look at footage from all the stores in his path.

Blu, sensing they really didn't have time for this, said, "Let's start at the other end. This guy isn't stupid."

And that's where they found the SUV he'd used.

All of them looked out from the store they were sitting in and found the SUV still there. His car. With his fingerprints.

Powers grabbed his radio as they all ran outside to it. He called in the plate number and came up with an address. The SUV was not reported stolen.

Blu and Crome ran back to his truck.

Powers protested but gave up and jumped in the backseat. While Blu drove, Crome punched the address into the truck's GPS. It was eight minutes away.

Harmony rammed into the door with her shoulder but it didn't budge. She did it again and felt her shoulder bruise. A voice from behind the door said, "Yes?"

It sounded like a groggy Maureen.

Harmony said, "Maureen! It's Harmony. We need to get out of here. I can't get your door open."

"Harmony? Is Mick with you?"

Harmony didn't want to spook her. She said, "He's on the way, but we need to get out of here. Is there anything you can use to help me get this door open?"

Harmony backed up and slammed all her weight into the door. It finally opened and Maureen, standing on shaking legs, looked confused.

Harmony grabbed her hand and pulled her. "Let's go."

Maureen seemed to struggle.

The man had a new plan now—cut his losses and run. Things were coming apart. Harmony was loose in the house. Carraway and Crome were now closer to finding out who he was than he preferred. He was hoping to toy with them some more before he got them to his house and killed the women in front of them. Now he'd have to settle for leaving their bodies to be found.

He opened the drawer in the hall cabinet where he kept one of his guns, a nine millimeter H&K. After feeding a full clip into it, he set off hunting the women, finding them exactly where he thought they'd be, trying to get out the back door.

Harmony had one of the wooden kitchen chairs raised, ready to break a window.

The man raised the pistol and aimed.

Mick Crome rounded the corner from the front of the house. In his hands was a large handgun that looked just like the forty-four the man had lost at Carraway's house. The biker pulled the trigger twice.

The man felt his body jerk back and slam into the wall behind him. For a split second, he lost half the feeling in his face before he felt nothing at all as he crashed to the floor.

Blu rounded the corner after Crome's second shot and caught the last glimpse of the man falling to the floor, a blood smear down the wall tracing his slide into the abyss. Crome looked at the man, as if waiting to make sure he was dead. When he didn't move, Crome went over to Maureen, who looked okay but was being supported by Harmony. The big forty-four Powers had given them back dropped to the floor.

Blu said, "I'll check the house for others."

Handing off Maureen to Crome, Harmony said, "I don't think there's anyone else here."

It was his experience to make sure. The last thing he needed was someone getting the drop on them.

Powers stormed through the open front door, the locked one Blu had picked open. He said, "You couldn't wait, could you?"

Harmony said, "If they'd have waited any longer, we'd be dead."

Blu didn't feel the need to add anything else.

Chapter Forty-Four

Blu stood outside the man's house. This had been about a case from the past, but not one he would have ever linked to anything. The question of why the man had chosen this time to go after him and Crome might not ever be answered.

Tess and Patricia showed up, along with Darcy and Brack. But no one could talk to Harmony or Maureen. The detectives were getting their statements.

While the nightmare kidnapping was over, the aftermath was a real mess.

Tess interrupted Blu's thoughts. "I did a quick background on him. The man's name was Casper Fields. He was head of an eco-terrorist group called Marine Life Marines. Great concept, poor execution, you ask me."

"MLM ECO?" Blu said. "Why now?"

"Because you guys made the news last year," said a female voice behind them.

They both turned around and saw Harmony.

Tess went up to her and gave her a hug.

"Where's Maureen?" Blu asked.

Harmony said, "With Crome."

Blu was glad she was okay and talking but still irritated about the whole thing.

Harmony said, "All I heard, over and over again, was how you two should not be allowed to harm others like you did someone named Grietje. I had a feeling she was his lover or something. But the guy was completely nuts."

"What about the mayor?" Blu asked.

"Unfortunately for him," Harmony said, "that was a bonus. He hated the mayor, too."

Blu said, "The mayor won the votes to get the Cruise Vessel Act passed. And cruise ships started coming into Charleston."

Tess asked, "How did the man even know to find you on the mayor's boat?"

Harmony, wearing green scrubs because the detectives had taken her clothes for evidence, said, "He was about to abduct me when he overheard me set up a meeting with Ron. It gave Fields enough time to beat us onto the boat. I knew the mayor had a reputation but I figured I could kick his butt if he tried anything. What I didn't figure was being attacked by Fields."

Blu said, "This was just a bad time to be in it for all of us. But especially Ms. Harmony here and Maureen."

Chapter Forty-Five

Sunday morning

Blu reread the front-page headline on the Sunday edition of the Palmetto Pulse one last time and dropped it, facing up on the coffee table in his living room. It read: Mayor Sails Last Cruise and it was coauthored by Harmony Childs, Darcy Pelton, and Tess Ray. Of course, Patricia published it as a sendoff for her empire.

Crome asked Blu if it was okay to take some time off and get Maureen out of town for a while. At first, Blu didn't know what to make of Crome's request. When the biker went on his three-year sabbatical, the only thing Blu got was a phone call from Key West with Crome saying he'd be gone for a while after he'd already been gone for a month.

As for Maureen, well, she'd need time to heal. She was a strong woman. She'd have to be to put up with Crome for any length of time, but the man Fields had tried his best to do a number on her. Only time would tell how she'd pull through.

Harmony's resilience came from the fact that she had overcome her assailant. Blu's take was she'd proven to herself that she could handle what life threw at her. God help her next man.

One of the few good things to come out of this tragedy was the article's exposure of their peeper source. While they didn't divulge their source directly, there were enough pictures of his house and camera system taken from the beach that left little doubt.

Blu dressed in his best button-down shirt and linen slacks and walked out to his truck. The horses, Dink and Doofus in particular, seemed to sense his trepidation and steered clear, eyeballing him from the water trough.

Hope, who had taken the job of office manager at Blu Carraway Investigations a little too seriously and had practically moved in to get the place organized, said, "Good luck, Dad."

He kissed the top of her head, gave the horses a wave, and drove away, steering his way toward North Charleston.

As he drove, he contemplated how many different ways this could go and settled on two. Both were scary, but for different reasons.

Because he hadn't given himself quite enough time to get to the Church of Redemption, Blu pulled into the rough asphalt parking lot five minutes after the service had started. He found a spot in the very back and locked his truck.

His phone vibrated in his pocket. It was Tess. Not the distraction he needed right now.

He let her call go to voicemail and walked to the recently renovated church. Brother Thomas had relocated with his flock as the tourist section of King Street continued past Calhoun Street. The Ravenel Bridge had been both a blessing and a curse depending on which part of the income chart people found themselves. While businesses had moved in, a lot of the people residing in the area had to move out. The tax value of their homes had increased and their landlords had decided to cash in.

The double doors on the white, clapboard-sided building opened easy enough given their heavy, all wood construction. Someone must be greasing the hinges. The church, air conditioned thank God, was packed. Everyone, mostly African Americans, stood facing the front. Brother Thomas, the church leader, was in his element while standing in front of them. Six-foot-three and three-hundred-and-fifty pounds, the man was a force to be reckoned with. Wearing his trademark black suit and minister's collar, he spoke about Jesus while a choir serenaded the congregation with background vocals.

It took Blu a few seconds to spot Billie in the choir. Even if he hadn't been able to pick her out, it wouldn't have mattered. After Brother Thomas finished speaking, she moved away from the rest of the choir. The preacher handed her his microphone and she began to sing a song Blu remembered her humming in the shower when they'd still been together, "All In" by the Chapel Band.

As the tempo built, the congregation began to dance around the church.

Blu wondered what he was doing here. Billie was with her family. He wasn't sure he could give her what she wanted and needed. They'd been working up to being together for twenty years and now everything he'd hoped would happen was falling apart in his mind.

The woman he loved had found God and Blu wasn't sure she'd accept him as he was. His relationship with God was sketchy at best. He believed, for sure. Over the course of the last year, Billie had gotten closer to her connection with Jesus and farther from Blu. He didn't resent it. She was a stronger person now than she'd ever been.

In the midst of everything going on around him, Blu realized he didn't belong here. These people were freely worshiping and he was intruding. He got up from his seat, ready to leave.

Brother Thomas blocked his exit and held out a hand. His black minister's suit and white collar took up what space there was in his seat row.

It was too loud to have a conversation so Blu nodded and took the offered hand. The preacher motioned for him to step outside, exactly where Blu was headed. In the lowcountry sunlight, Brother Thomas said, "Good to see you, Brother Blu."

Not sure what to say, Blu said, "You, too."

"Billie sure sing like a bird, don't she?"

The one thing about Brother Thomas that Blu had learned was not to underestimate the man. His simple words had tricked better people than Blu into thinking they were dealing with some yokel.

"She sure does," Blu said. "I missed hearing her voice."

"She miss you, too." He gave Blu a sympathetic smile, which normally would seem odd on the three-hundred-and-fifty pound man who matched Blu's six-three height, and put a hand on his shoulder. "She tol' me she wanted to see you again and here you is."

Blu looked away, unsure what to do. "I wondered if I'd see her again, too."

"You're a good man, Blu Carraway. Don't let the enemy tell you different. Billie ain't no naïve teenage girl with a crush. She a grown woman with a good head on her shoulders." He paused, then said, "And she love you, son."

With that, Blu met the Preacher's gaze.

Brother Thomas said, "Don't take my word for it. Come back inside and talk to her after the service. She'll tell you herself."

"I, um," Blu began, measured his words, and said, "I was about to leave."

"I know. Still can, if that's what you want."

Blu thought about Maureen and Harmony and what happened to his daughter two years ago. He thought about how his partner reacted when he found out Maureen was in trouble. There was no doubt in his mind he would have gone off the rails just like Crome did if a woman he cared deeply about was taken. He didn't want that for Billie or Crome or any of his friends.

He extended a hand to the preacher. "I'd appreciate if you didn't tell her I was here, Brother."

The preacher shook his hand. "You are always welcome in God's house. Ain't no such thing as a bad time to be in it here."

Walking back to his truck, Blu did his best to ignore Brother Thomas' last words, especially how they mimicked his own but with a positive spin. He loosened his tie and thought about the biggest mistake he had ever made in his life and wondered if this was it.

DAVID BURNSWORTH

David Burnsworth became fascinated with the Deep South at a young age. After a degree in Mechanical Engineering from the University of Tennessee and fifteen years in the corporate world, he made the decision to write a novel. He is the author of both the Brack Pelton and the Blu Carraway Mystery Series. Having lived in Charleston on Sullivan's Island for five years, the setting was a foregone conclusion. He and his wife call South Carolina home.

Books by David Burnsworth

The Blu Carraway Mystery Series

BLU HEAT (Prequel Novella)
IN IT FOR THE MONEY (#1)
BAD TIME TO BE IN IT (#2)

The Brack Pelton Mystery Series

SOUTHERN HEAT (#1)
BURNING HEAT (#2)
BIG CITY HEAT (#3)

Henery Press Mystery Books

And finally, before you go...
Here are a few other mysteries
you might enjoy:

NUN TOO SOON

Alice Loweecey

A Giulia Driscoll Mystery (#1)

Giulia Falcone-Driscoll has just taken on her first impossible client:
The Silk Tie Killer. He's hired Driscoll Investigations to prove his
innocence with only thirteen days to accomplish it. Everyone in
town is sure Roger Fitch strangled his girlfriend with one of his silk
neckties. On top of all that, her assistant's first baby is due any
second, her scary smart admin still doesn't relate well to humans,
and her police detective husband insists her client is guilty.

Giulia's ownership of Driscoll Investigations hasn't changed her
passion for justice from her convent years. But the more dirt she
digs up, the more she's worried her efforts will help a murderer
escape. As the client accuses DI of dragging its heels on purpose,
Giulia thinks The Silk Tie Killer might be choosing one of his ties
for her own neck.

Available at booksellers nationwide and online

Visit www.henerypress.com for details

BOARD STIFF
Kendel Lynn

An Elliott Lisbon Mystery (#1)

As director of the Ballantyne Foundation on Sea Pine Island, SC, Elliott Lisbon scratches her detective itch by performing discreet inquiries for Foundation donors. Usually nothing more serious than retrieving a pilfered Pomeranian. Until Jane Hatting, Ballantyne board chair, is accused of murder. The Ballantyne's reputation tanks, Jane's headed to a jail cell, and Elliott's sexy ex is the new lieutenant in town.

Armed with moxie and her Mini Coop, Elliott uncovers a trail of blackmail schemes, gambling debts, illicit affairs, and investment scams. But the deeper she digs to clear Jane's name, the guiltier Jane looks. The closer she gets to the truth, the more treacherous her investigation becomes. With victims piling up faster than shells at a clambake, Elliott realizes she's next on the killer's list.

Available at booksellers nationwide and online

Visit www.henerypress.com for details

SHADOW OF DOUBT

Nancy Cole Silverman

A Carol Childs Mystery (#1)

When a top Hollywood Agent is found poisoned in her home, suspicion quickly turns to one of her two nieces. But Carol Childs, a reporter for a local talk radio station doesn't believe it. The suspect is her neighbor and friend, and also her primary source for insider industry news. When a media frenzy pits one niece against the other—and the body count starts to rise—Carol knows she must save her friend from being tried in courts of public opinion.

But even the most seasoned reporter can be surprised, and when a Hollywood psychic shows warns Carol there will be more deaths, things take an unexpected turn. Suddenly nobody is above suspicion. Carol must challenge both her friendship and the facts, and the only thing she knows for certain is the killer is still out there and the closer she gets to the truth, the more danger she's in.

Available at booksellers nationwide and online

Visit www.henerypress.com for details

PROTOCOL
Kathleen Valenti

A Maggie O'Malley (#1)

Freshly minted college graduate Maggie O'Malley embarks on a career fueled by professional ambition and a desire to escape the past. As a pharmaceutical researcher, she's determined to save lives from the shelter of her lab. But on her very first day she's pulled into a world of uncertainty. Reminders appear on her phone for meetings she's never scheduled with people she's never met. People who end up dead.

With help from her best friend, Maggie discovers the victims on her phone are connected to each other and her new employer. She soon unearths a treacherous plot that threatens her mission—and her life. Maggie must unlock deadly secrets to stop horrific abuses of power before death comes calling for her.

Available at booksellers nationwide and online

Visit www.henerypress.com for details

CPSIA information can be obtained
at www.ICGtesting.com
Printed in the USA
FFOW01n0948080618
47062242-49419FF

9 781635 113587